Cold Spring
Harbor

RICHARD YATES

Cold Spring Harbor

DELACORTE PRESS/SEYMOUR LAWRENCE

Published by Delacorte Press/Seymour Lawrence
1 Dag Hammarskjold Plaza
New York, N.Y. 10017

Library of Congress Cataloging in Publication Data

Yates, Richard, 1926–
  Cold Spring Harbor.

  I. Title.
PS3575.A83C65 1986   813'.54
ISBN 0-385-29502-2
Library of Congress Catalog Card Number: 86-2095

For Kurt Vonnegut

Cold Spring
Harbor

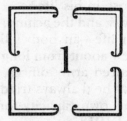

1

All the sorrows of Evan Shepard's loutish adolescence were redeemed at seventeen, in 1935, when he fell in love with automobiles. His persistent bullying of weaker boys, his thick-witted ways of offending girls, his inept and embarrassing ventures into petty crime—none of those things mattered any more, except as bad memories. He had found a high romance in driving fast and far, over most of Long Island, and he soon attained intimacy with the mechanical parts of any car he could get his hands on. For whole days at a time, meticulously taking a car apart or putting it together in the dust of his parents' driveway, Evan would be lost to the world.

And it was always a pleasure for his father, Charles Shepard, just to stand at a window and watch him working alone out there in the sun. Nobody could have guessed a year ago that this particular boy would ever learn to organize and focus his mind on a useful job of work; and wasn't that the beginning of maturity? Wasn't it what helped a man develop will and purpose in his life?

Well, of course it was; and the aching, crying need for will and purpose in your life—anybody's life—was something Charles Shepard knew about from long and helpless experience. He was a retired army officer, a man with poetic habits of thought that he'd always tried to suppress, and it often seemed that his own capacity for zeal had vanished with the Armistice of 1918.

As an impassioned young second lieutenant of infantry, newly married to the prettiest girl at the officers' club dance and reasonably sure she would pray for him, he had arrived in France three days after the war ended—and his disappointment was so intense that more than a few other officers had to tell him, impatiently, not to be silly about it.

"I'm *not,*" he would insist, "I'm *not.*" But he always knew there'd be no escaping the truth; he had even begun to suspect that a queasy sense of abortion might haunt the rest of his life.

"Apart from knowing I'll love you forever," he wrote to his wife from Le Havre, "I seem to have lost confidence in just about everything else. I've come to believe that only a very, very few matters in the world can ever be trusted to make sense."

Back in the States again and surrounded by whooping, hollering men who could scarcely wait to be out of the army, Charles came to an abrupt and unpopular decision. For reasons never entirely clear to himself, he signed up to stay in.

One way he could always tell the reasons weren't clear was that he had to keep going over and over them in his mind for years, as if they were answers in a dim little three-part catechism: the army could almost be seen as a vocation; it provided the security that a married man and a father would always need; and there might, eventually, be another war.

He served as a first lieutenant long enough to make him worry about being the oldest first lieutenant anyone knew, and almost all of his duties in those years, greatly against his wishes, lay in the heavy tedium of office work.

Fort Devens, Fort Dix, Fort Benning, Fort Meade—every army post made brave attempts to be different from the others, but they were all the same. They were as plain as hell, and they were built on the assumption of obedience. Even in the closely guarded privacy of Married Officers' Housing, and even at night, you could never forget where you were, or why, and neither could your wife. If everything in both your lives was expected to conform to the boundaries of a peacetime military preserve, and if your wife was as bright and spirited a girl as Grace Shepard, you could never honestly say you were surprised—frightened, certainly, but not surprised—when her nerves gave way and fell apart.

From the time of her first hospitalization Charles knew he had better make what plans he could for getting out of the army soon—and by then there was another trouble that suggested he'd be out of it soon enough anyway: his eyesight had gone rapidly bad and was getting worse. Ironically, though, it was during that same year that the army gave him something interesting to do. On being promoted to captain at last, he was placed in command of a rifle company.

And oh, he liked those two hundred men—even the misfits; even the soreheads. After a very few weeks he was proud of them, and proud of seeming to have earned their respect. He savored those moments of every day that encouraged him to believe he was looking after them, taking care of them, and to believe they knew it; and he never tired of hearing them say "the captain," or "the company commander."

When he took them out on long marches, under full field equipment, he liked the rhythm and the sweat and the disciplined pain of it, even though he might not always be sure he could make the distance. And there were other times, squinting and peering into their opened, empty Springfield rifles, while the men themselves stood unnaturally straight and perfectly still in formation, with perfectly expressionless faces, when he would find himself wishing he could lead this company into some fanciful war of his own imagining. Nearly all of them would distinguish themselves in the field because nearly every action there would be above and beyond the call of duty; then when the war was over their dead would come back to life again, just in time for the drinking and the laughter and the pretty girls.

If Grace had made a full recovery he might have tried to fake his way through any number of eye tests, just to stay with the company as long as possible, but there was no such luck. She had a second breakdown, and this time he knew he couldn't hesitate any longer. Even before she was out of the hospital he had made arrangements to resign his commission.

For several days, as they sorted out and packed their belongings, Charles toyed with the idea of moving to some place that neither of them had ever seen—California, say, or Canada—where they might both be rejuvenated in the bravery of starting a new life. But then, earlier Shepards had always been Long Island people, accustomed to grassy plains and potato farms and a wind smelling faintly of salt water, and so the more sensible thing was to go home. On the strength of his small but adequate retirement pension he bought a small but adequate brown frame house on the north shore, at the edge of the village of Cold Spring Harbor.

Before very long he was known around the village as a dignified, courteous man who always did his family's grocery shopping, and took care of their laundry, because his wife was said to be an invalid. There were hesitant, groundless rumors that he'd been a hero in the war, or that he'd served with some other kind of brilliance; people might have been surprised to learn that he'd retired as a captain because his appearance and bearing were more in the style of a colonel: you could picture him taking salutes from a battalion or a whole regiment of men and sternly watching them pass in review. That impression might take on a faintly comic aspect sometimes, when you saw him wrestle and grapple on the street with grocery bags, or with laundry bags, his gray hair blown awry and his thick glasses beginning to slip down his nose; but nobody, even in the tavern, ever made jokes about him.

"I'm back, dear," he called to Grace one afternoon, easing a great burden of groceries onto the kitchen table, and he continued talking to her in the same raised voice as he went about the business of putting things away where they belonged. "I think Evan's been out there working on that engine for about ten hours straight," he called. "I don't know where he gets the energy. *Or* the diligence."

When he'd finished with the groceries he broke out some ice and fixed two drinks of bourbon and water, one with a double shot of whiskey. He carried them into the living room and out onto a heavily shaded sun porch, where Grace reclined on a chaise longue, and he carefully put the one with the double bourbon into her waiting, reaching hand.

"Isn't it remarkable how a boy can change? Just in a few months' time?" he asked her as he sat with his own drink on a straight chair, close beside her. The day had been tiring but he could rest for half an hour now, until it was time to get dinner started.

At certain moments, if the light and the alcohol worked to her advantage, Grace could still be the prettiest girl at the officers' club dance. Charles had learned to wait for those moments with a lover's patience, and to cherish them when they came, but they'd grown increasingly rare. Most of the time—this afternoon, for example—he found he would rather not look at her at all because she would only look ruined: heavy, dissatisfied, apparently grieving in silence for the loss of herself.

A kindly, aging army doctor at Fort Meade, in discussing her condition, had once made use of the word "neurasthenia"—and Charles, after looking it up in the dictionary, had decided it was something he could live with. But later, in New York, a much younger civilian doctor had dismissed that term as being too old-fashioned and imprecise to have any value in modern medicine. Then, like an overconfident salesman, this younger man had begun to press for what he called "a course of psychotherapy."

"Well, if we're going to argue about words, Doctor," Charles said, barely keeping his temper, "I'll have to tell you that I have no confidence in any word beginning with 'psych.' I don't think you people know what you're doing in that funny, shifty field, and I don't think you ever will."

And he'd never been sorry he'd said that, or that he'd gotten up and walked out of the office a minute later, even though it gave the doctor permission to sit there looking as piqued and vain, as dirty-minded and victorious as a portrait photograph of Sigmund Freud himself. Some things you did were worth regretting; others not.

Not very long ago, during the worst of his son's difficulties, Charles had found himself unable to prevent the insidious current of psychiatric jargon from beginning to flow again, here in his own house, as various people urged him to "get professional help" for Evan, or to "look into professional counselling" for him; and the funny part now was that he could remember being halfway tempted to go along with that kind of talk, if only because all other talk at the time had been so much more unsettling—talk of police probation and of juvenile court, even talk of reform school. Those were days when it often seemed there would always be a stranger's angry voice on the phone, complaining about Evan, or a couple of cops at the door.

Well, it certainly was remarkable how a boy could change. And maybe things like this really did get better of their own accord, if you gave them time; maybe all you could ever do, beyond suffering, was wait and see what might be going to happen next.

From this sun porch, by leaning a little forward in his chair and looking out through an unshaded section of one window, even a man with weak vision could see the outlines of Evan Shepard concluding his day's work in the driveway —putting tools away, tiredly straightening his spine, wiping his hands on a clean rag.

"And you know what else is really surprising, dear?" Charles said. "About Evan? He *looks* so much better. In the face, I mean. I don't think we could ever have expected it, but he's turning into a very—an extremely good-looking young man."

"Oh, I know," Grace Shepard said, using her voice for the first time all day, and smiling for the first time too. "Oh, yes, I know. He certainly is."

And they could both sense that they weren't the only observers to have noticed that.

2

Girls, even those who'd been revolted by the very sight of Evan Shepard a year ago, were beginning to agree among themselves that he was handsome; and there was at least one girl who'd thought he was handsome all along, whether she'd ever confided it to her friends or not.

Mary Donovan was a slender girl with rich, loose, dark red hair and the kind of pretty face that other girls called "saucy," and she had been secretly partial to Evan Shepard since the seventh grade. It had made her feel awful to hear about any of his troubles—the time he'd laid open a younger boy's scalp with a brick; the time the police had booked him on a charge of disorderly conduct and locked him up for the night "to teach him a lesson"; the time he'd broken into a hardware store and been caught at the drawer of the cash register—and she may have been the first person in Cold Spring Harbor, apart from his parents, to care about the profound improvements that seemed to have begun in him all at once.

Mary had always assumed she would have an athlete for a lover—why not?—and so she found it slightly disappointing that Evan wasn't athletic, though he looked strong and nimble enough for any team. Still, she soon discovered there were thrilling things to see—things to watch—in the very way he handled his car. Spraying gravel as he gunned away from school every afternoon, he would pull up short at the edge of the highway, craning his fine profile to watch and wait for an opening in the traffic, often with a light wind ruffling his wavy black hair; then he'd make a wide, swift, wonderfully confident turn into the right lane and take off, moaning away as far into the distance as her eyes could see, and beyond that. He was a boy born to drive, and in the heart of at least one girl he made driving into the equivalent of a spectator sport.

Standing alone to gaze after him, with her schoolbooks hugged at her breasts because that was the way all the other girls carried them, she began to understand that her life would never be the same.

On some nights, lying awake and restless in her fragrant bedroom, Mary Donovan would find it necessary to submit to make-believe. She would pretend that her own hands were those of Evan Shepard, and she'd allow them to roam and fondle various parts of herself, taking their time, having their way with her, until the sweet tension was almost unbearable; then at last she'd achieve the spasm and the helpless little cry that meant she could probably fall asleep. And when she saw Evan Shepard at school in the morning, after one of those nights, she would blush and feel almost as mortified as if he knew her secret and might tell everybody.

One autumn afternoon in a heavily echoing high-school corridor, when they were both seniors, Evan found the courage to ask Mary if she'd like to go to the movies, and she said okay.

After the show that night they sat clasping and kissing like young movie stars, in the moonlit privacy of his parked car, until Mary drew away from him with a little pout of promise. She worked and shrugged her way free of her upper clothing and let it fall around her waist; then she put both hands behind her to unfasten her brassiere, and when she'd shucked it off she gave him an uncertain look, as if to ask if she'd done the right thing.

"Oh," he said in a voice hushed with reverence. "Oh, you're nice. Oh, you're really nice, Mary."

With one lovely tit in his hand and the other unbelievably in his mouth, he knew now, from the incessant talk of other boys, that the next thing to do was use his free hand for trying to "get into her pants." But he'd scarcely begun that move when Mary surprised him again. Squirming, she re-arranged herself and shyly opened her legs to make it easier for him.

"Oh, Evan," she said. "Oh, Evan."

Very soon, then, in whispered agreement, they pulled themselves briefly together, got out of the front seat for a moment's painful deprivation, and sank voluptuously into the back.

Love may not be everything in the world, but neither of them gave that possibility a moment's thought until after they were married. It was a marriage that might have occurred much later, when they were both a few years older, if Mary hadn't found she was pregnant in the very early months of their romance. Then their parents had to be told, and plans had to be made in something of a hurry. A

modest wedding was arranged, a small two-room apartment was found and rented in the adjacent commercial
town of Huntington, and a friend of Mary's father was able
to secure a job for Evan at a machine-tool factory twenty
miles away. It was unskilled work, at apprentice wages, but
there was reason to hope that Evan's mechanical ability
might soon be recognized there; and it was certainly better
than no job at all.

The baby was a girl, named Kathleen after Mary's grandmother. A conscientious number of family snapshots were
taken, and in all but one the camera caught Evan and Mary
wearing smiles of theatrical intensity. The single exception,
soon thrown away, showed both of them looking as scared
and desperate as if they'd rather be anywhere else, doing
anything else than having to pose for that photograph.

By now the adults of both families could subside into
their own concerns again; but they must all have known,
though nobody put it into words, that adolescent marriages
aren't likely to last.

Evan began taking long, aimless drives alone at night, so
he could frown in the darkness and think. It was an excellent thing to have a pretty girl being crazy about you all the
time—there was no denying that. Still, it could leave you
wondering. Was this all there was ever going to be? And he
would sock the steering wheel with the soft part of his fist,
again and again, because he couldn't believe his life had
become so fixed and settled before he'd even turned nineteen.

Mary wasn't happy either. There had to be high school,
of course, so you could learn about boys and love and all
that; but then there was supposed to be college too, for
four years, and after college there was supposed to be a
time of living in New York and having a job and buying nice
clothes and going to parties and meeting a few—well, meet-

ing a few interesting people. Wasn't that so? And didn't everybody know it?

Oh, if it weren't for the burden of knowing Evan adored her, that he'd be terribly lost without her—if it weren't for that, she knew she would now be putting her mind to finding some way out of all this.

Sometimes, confronting her daughter's round, lovely eyes while lifting her out of the crib, or out of the bath, Mary would find she had to will her own face into an expression of kindness because she was afraid even an infant might recognize the looks of resentment and blame.

When the quarrels began they were long and harsh and self-renewing.

"Are you ever going to let me be a person, Evan?"

"How do you mean, 'a person?' "

"Oh, you know. Or if you don't know there's no point in my trying to explain it."

"Well, but I mean how do you mean 'let' you? Seems to me you can be any kind of a person you want, any time."

"Oh, God; never mind. You'd know perfectly well what I'm trying to say if you could ever picture me away from this stove, or away from this sink, or out of that bed."

"Oh. So is this going to be the kind of talk where we stay up half the night until our lips are all dry and cracked and we can't even get laid? Because if that's the deal one more time you'd better count me out. I'm tired, is all. You can't even imagine how tired I am."

"*You're* tired. *You're* tired. Listen, mister factory apprentice, I'm so tired I could scream."

"Well, but what the hell else do you *want,* Mary? You want to get out and meet other guys? Is that it? You want to open your *legs* for other guys? Because I've got news for you, sweetheart: I'm dumb; I'm dumb; but I'm not *that* fucking dumb."

"Oh, if only you knew, Evan. If only you had an inkling of how dumb you really are."

"Yeah? Yeah?"

"Yeah."

But by the time they did break up, a year and a half after the wedding, there was no quarrelling at all. In the plainness of their need to get out of that Huntington apartment and away from each other, fast, they both seemed to know that any further quarrels would be as embarrassing as losing your temper at a stranger in a public place.

Mary enrolled as a freshman at Long Island University, after arranging for her parents to take care of the baby, and within six months she was said to be engaged to a pre-dental student from Hempstead.

Evan moved back into his parents' house and went on working at the machine-tool plant. He didn't know what else to do, and nobody near him came up with any better ideas—though his father did try to offer encouraging advice of a general kind.

"Well, Evan, this is bound to be a difficult time for you," he said one night as they lingered at the dinner table after Grace had gone upstairs. "But I think you'll find that sometimes things do get better of their own accord. It may be that all you can do now, apart from trying to keep your spirits up, is wait and see what's going to happen next."

3

A celebrated clinic of optometry was opened for business in 1941, in lower Manhattan, where people suffering from very poor vision could be equipped with spectacles said to bring about remarkable improvements in their daily lives.

Charles Shepard made an appointment at the place as soon as he found out about it, in April of that year; then, rather than go into New York alone on the train, he asked his son to drive him there.

"Well, but I'll lose a day's pay," Evan said, as Charles had expected he would, and Charles had just the right answer ready, for delivery in just the right kind of quiet voice.

"That doesn't matter," he told him, "and what's more, you know it doesn't matter."

Evan looked briefly puzzled, but then he seemed to understand—or seemed at least to see that this might be a trip worth taking if the old man had something on his mind.

He was twenty-three now, still working in the factory and living in his parents' house, and his father had long suspected he was following the course of least resistance: to break out of it would have required ambition, and there didn't yet seem to be a trace of that quality in his character. Delinquency may once have threatened to possess the boy, but now a pure lassitude was gathering to engulf the man. He was getting more dramatically handsome all the time, too—girls gave him startled looks of helplessness wherever he went—and that was the funny part: it didn't seem right for anyone so splendid-looking to have so little going on in his head.

Charles had often wished they could have an unhurried, serious talk, as other fathers and sons were said to do, but there never seemed to be time for that at home: as soon as Evan cleared away his dinner dishes he'd be out in his car and gone, often for most of the night. Charles didn't know where he went on those drives, or what he did, and he was sometimes vaguely envious, imagining easy romantic adventures all around Long Island and New York; but then he'd wonder, sadly, if Evan's carousing might amount to nothing more than wasting time at the same roadside barroom night after night, in the drink-fuddled company of other factory employees as indolent as he was. And wouldn't that be only natural? If you lived like a proletarian long enough, among proletarians, weren't you almost certain to become a proletarian too?

That was why the day of the eye clinic had become extremely important for Charles. Given an hour or two alone with Evan on the drive into lower Manhattan, and an hour or two more on the drive back, there was every reason to hope their talk might be profitable, as well as serious.

They set out at noon, in mild and pretty spring weather,

and Charles was able to get his part of the talk started after a very few miles.

"Memory's a curious thing," he began, and he was afraid at once that this might be a weak, dead-giveaway kind of opening line, like the first sentence of a radio commercial, but he didn't stop. "I don't suppose you can remember much about Fort Benning, Georgia, can you?"

"Oh, a little, yeah," Evan said. "I remember a few things."

"Well, you were still pretty small then, but that time at Benning's been on my mind a lot lately. Your mother and I had these great—"

He spoke carefully, listening to the words as they came and trying as hard as an actor not to let them sound rehearsed, though in fact they were: he had rehearsed the whole of this speech last night in whispers, in bed, right down to the pauses where Evan could make a comment or two. Striving in every breath for the illusion of spontaneity, he was only reciting material he knew by heart.

"Your mother and I had these great friends in those years, Joe and Nancy Raymond. Do you remember them at all? Had a girl of about your age and a younger boy?"

"Yeah, I do," Evan said. "I mean, I do now."

"We took to spending an awful lot of time together, in our place or theirs, or down at the club, and we never seemed to get tired of each others' company. Then one night Joe told us he'd decided to resign his commission. Said he wanted to find out what making money would be like. He'd been looking into the sales end of the radio business—radio was still brand-new then, you see, and people were saying it was a field with an unlimited future. His idea was to get started selling for one of the manufacturers, Philco or Majestic or one of the others, then move over into the management side and go on up from there.

"Well, naturally, your mother and I felt bad. We'd be

losing our best friends—really the only friends we had, at the time—and I can remember your mother saying 'What're we going to *do* without you?'

"And here's what I've been leading up to, Evan: Joe Raymond asked me to go along with him. He said we'd probably starve for a year or two, or three, but he said once we got our bearings we'd begin to move forward and nothing in the world would ever stop us. Then your mother spoke up again and said 'Oh, let's *do* it, Charles.'

"And I'm afraid I can never forget what happened after that. I'll always remember how crestfallen, how disappointed she looked when I started making excuses and shying away from it, backing down, trying to laugh it off by saying I couldn't picture myself as a salesman, and that kind of thing. I felt like a coward, and I think that's probably because I *was* a coward. I simply didn't have Joe Raymond's spirit, or Joe Raymond's guts.

"Well, I can't tell you what became of the Raymonds because we lost touch with them after a while, the way people always seem to do, even with dear friends. I don't know whether Joe ever did get ahead in business or whether he went down and out in the Depression. But I'll tell you this much, Evan: years later, after your mother's illness, I would've given anything to take it all back. Time and again over the years I've wanted to go back to that night at Fort Benning and say 'Right; good; me too. That's what we'll do, Joe. We'll get out and sell radios.' "

Charles's voice had grown a little more intense than he'd meant it to, so he waited a few seconds to bring his breathing back to normal. Then he said "I think you can probably guess why I wanted to tell you about this, Evan. It's because I really don't like the way things are sort of idling and drifting for you these days. I don't like the kind of job you have; I don't like your living at home instead of off somewhere else by yourself. You'll be twenty-four soon, and it seems to me you ought to be taking command of your life. What I'm trying to say is, I'd like you to be a little more like Joe Raymond, if that's possible, and a little less like me. Do you understand this at all?"

"Well, I think so, yes," Evan said. "Yes. Sure, I understand."

And Charles, tired of talking, felt a tentative sense of having done his best. The only part of it he regretted now was "you ought to be taking command of your life," because that might have a faintly sanctimonious ring for a boy who'd been told only a few years ago that things were likely to get better of their own accord. Well, never mind. The phrasing may not have been perfect, but the message was clear.

If a long silence had developed in the car now it was only because Evan felt he needed time to prepare a full and appropriate reply. He wanted to tell of ideas he hadn't yet quite worked out in his own mind, so there was a lot of material to be organized before he started talking; besides, he was aware that too abrupt an announcement might spoil the drama of his father's confession.

"As a matter of fact, Dad," he began when he was ready, "I've been making a few plans that I guess I probably should've discussed with you."

And with a shyness in his voice that surprised him, because he hadn't meant to be shy about this, he said he wanted to go to college and study mechanical engineering. Oh, it would take some doing—he'd never really graduated from high school, for one thing, and the money part would certainly be a problem too, unless he could somehow qualify for a scholarship—but once those matters were cleared up he knew he could handle the rest of it. He had already sent away for several catalogues.

"Well, Evan," Charles said, "that's marvelous. I'm delighted to know you've been thinking along those lines. I won't be able to help you out much on the financial side, as you know, but I'll back you up in any way I can."

They had scarcely reached Queens, but the skin on the back of Evan's neck and along his forearms had all turned to gooseflesh, just from hearing his father say "Well, Evan, that's marvelous." By the time they went across the Queensborough Bridge Evan had begun to feel like a young pioneer, like a courageous man, like the very kind of man his father might always have wanted him to be, and from there on the ride might as well have been something in a dream: across town and then swiftly down toward lower Manhattan, where Charles might find a pair of glasses that would bring about remarkable improvements in his daily life.

Somewhere below Forty-second Street it started to rain, and by the time they reached Twenty-third it was almost a downpour. Then just below Fourteenth Street, while Evan was taking what appeared to be an easy way through the long crooked maze of Greenwich Village, there was a thumping disturbance in the engine—he barely managed to pull over to the curb before it rattled and died.

"Doesn't sound very good," he said.

"No."

On getting out of the car and lifting the hood, Evan would have thought he knew this engine as well as he knew anything; but now, as it popped and hissed under his scrutiny and his gingerly prodding fingers, it had taken on the look and feel of something he would never understand.

"Well, it's a very old car," Charles said, standing in the street beside him and wearing a wrinkled raincoat that he'd found in the back seat. "These things happen. I think we'd better find a garage if we can, don't you?"

But neither of them knew this part of the city. There might not be a garage for miles around, and they walked two or three blocks without even finding a telephone booth. Charles guessed they would have to impose on somebody, and that was a nuisance—he had never liked going through the elaborate apologies and thanks it always entailed—but he pressed a random doorbell in the vestibule of a small, random apartment building.

"I'm terribly sorry," he said to the woman who opened the door, "but we've had some trouble with our car; I wonder if we could use your phone for just a minute."

"Well, of course," she said. "Please come in." She stepped back to welcome them into her sad living room, which smelled of cat droppings and cosmetics and recent cooking, and Charles had her figured at once as a nice person down on her luck. New York was honeycombed with this kind of wretched gentility.

"You're very kind," he told her. "Thank you so much. This shouldn't take long."

"Well, I'm glad we can help. Will you need this?"

The classified phone book she thrust at him was useless —he hadn't been able to bring that kind of print into focus for years—but he thumbed the pages of it anyway, standing at her telephone table, because that was easier than looking into her face. He could feel her watching him, and he could feel the weight of her wish that this chance encounter might develop into a happy little social occasion.

"Well," he said, "I'm afraid my eyes aren't very—Evan? Can you give me a hand with this?"

Evan had followed him into the room, blinking in embarrassment under the woman's smile; now he took over the phone book and found a place called West Village Motors that looked about right, and he crouched at the phone to dial the number.

"Won't you both sit down?" the woman said. "If you don't have to rush off?"

And there was no point in their rushing off now because it might take the mechanic half an hour or more to get here;

then, just before sitting down, it seemed only civil to introduce themselves, like guests at the beginning of an awkward party. The woman's name was Gloria Drake.

"Well, of course I don't drive," she said when the three of
them were seated, "so I've never understood anything
about cars, but I know they're terribly complicated—*and*
terribly dangerous." Here she gave a little laughing shud-
der that was probably meant to be girlish and disarming,
but all it did was call attention to how loose and ill-defined
her lips were. When she laughed and shuddered that way,
holding her shoulders high for emphasis, she looked like a
shuddering clown.

". . . Oh, I *know* Cold Spring Harbor," she cried a minute later. "Well, I suppose I shouldn't say I 'know' it, but
the children and I did spend a few days near there years
ago. And I'll never forget how lovely that part of the north
shore is: we were there in the fall, when all the leaves were
just beginning to turn. Oh, and I loved the Sound. I loved
Long Island Sound. Are you sure you wouldn't like some
sherry?"

She may not have been more than fifty, but there wasn't
much left of whatever she'd had in the way of looks. Her
hair was a blend of faded yellow and light gray, as if dyed by
many years of drifting cigarette smoke, and although you
could say she'd kept her figure, it was such a frail, slack little
figure that you couldn't picture it doing anything but sitting
right here, on this coffee-stained sofa. Her very way of
sitting suggested an anxious need to be heard and understood, and to be liked if possible: hunched forward with her
forearms on her knees and her clasped hands writhing to
the rhythms of her own talk.

Later, Charles Shepard would have to remind himself
that he'd probably done his share of the talking—he must
have given enough information and asked enough questions to keep her fuelled and going—but at the time, and

again in memory, it seemed that the afternoon was given over to Gloria Drake's voice: the long runs of it, the little bursts and hesitations of it, the hoarse, cigarette-heavy laughter in it, and the incipient hysteria. She was ready to give her heart away to total strangers off the street.

". . . Oh, my, no; we've only been in this funny place a few months; this is just temporary. But then we've always moved around a lot: the children were saying just the other day they've lost count of all the different houses and apartments we've had. Can't remember how many places, or even how many towns; isn't that remarkable? No, we've always been very restless, you see. I suppose you could say we're vagabonds at heart."

Charles and Evan had each accepted a deep glass of sherry some minutes ago, and Evan was discovering he liked the taste of it. This wasn't really so bad, goofing around Greenwich Village with your father. Even if some West Village Motors mechanic could fix the car they would probably miss the eye-clinic appointment now, and so the day would be wasted; but weren't there pleasures to be taken, sometimes, in a wasted day? Father and son could hit a few of the bars in this arty part of town; they might even get looped together, telling jokes and laughing, knowing they could catch a little sleep on the train going home.

". . . Oh, I do hope you can stay long enough to meet the children," Gloria Drake was saying. "They really should've been home by now; I can't imagine what's keeping them. They had to take our fine cat Perkins to the cat doctor, you see, because he's been throwing up all over the place . . ."

Once Charles risked a glance at Evan, as her voice rumbled on and on, and they were able to exchange quick winks that she couldn't have seen. Telling them about the cat reminded her of another, much earlier cat she'd once had—"Oh, this was long, long ago, when the children were small"—and that story required her to mention, in passing, that she'd been divorced for many years.

It came as no surprise to either of her listeners. Wives didn't often talk this way—even unhappy wives—and neither did widows. The Shepards were both ready to believe, this afternoon, that only a long-divorced woman would ever talk as if talking were sustenance, talk until veins the size of earthworms stood out in her temples, talk until little white beads of spit were gathered and working on each other near the corners of her mouth.

". . . Well, yes, and of course it's never been easy," she was saying, "with two children to raise entirely alone. I sort of—live by my wits, you see."

Charles had always thought "living by your wits" meant having some nimble if haphazard way of earning money, so he said "Oh? What kind of work is it you do, then, Mrs. Drake?" But he was sorry at once, because her own interpretation of the phrase had nothing to do with earning, or with work.

"Well, as I say"— and here the clownish look came briefly back into her face—"as I say, it's mostly been a matter of living from month to month, living from day to day; but we manage."

So she probably lived on alimony, and there was certainly nothing the matter with that; still, it might have been nicer if she hadn't tried to pretend it wasn't so.

". . . Oh, *there* they are," she cried, bolting to her feet at the sound of the doorbell. "My, I was beginning to worry." To pantomime "worry" she made as if to put her hand on her heart, but instead it cupped and clasped her pendulous left breast, as if she were feeling herself up, and that seemed funny enough to provoke another couple of winks as soon as her back was turned.

Gloria Drake's children were a boy just getting into adolescence and a girl just getting out of it. They both looked as frail as she was, suggesting that nobody in this family would ever be strong, but the girl had learned to carry it off in a surprisingly pretty way.

"Isn't this nice?" their mother demanded of them. "These gentlemen had some trouble with their car and they happened to ring our bell, you see, and now we've been having a *won*derful time . . ."

The girl's name was Rachel, and when she came up to shake hands with Evan she looked stricken. It lasted only a heartbeat or two before she smiled politely, but Evan had caught it, and could tell she'd seen him catch it. There might still be times in Evan Shepard's life when he was afraid he wouldn't amount to much, but he always knew what he looked like, and he knew it gave him a decided advantage with girls.

Soon the sherry was flowing again for everyone except the boy, Phil, a melancholy kid who didn't seem to mind being left out. He was fooling around on the floor with the cat. Rachel had taken a chair some distance away from Evan's, almost as though she didn't trust herself to be any closer, and he looked her over carefully as she exchanged a few courtesies with his father. He liked her skin and her brown hair and wide brown eyes. Nobody would ever call her "saucy"; still, everybody knew there were thousands of kinds of prettiness in girls; and besides, with this particular girl you didn't think of kinds or categories. She was herself: a little thin and soft, but with a wonderful look of having newly come to life. His mind began to play with the implications of words like "tender" and "fresh" and "perishable"; this was a girl you could cherish and protect. And the best part was that he knew it would be easy to come back to this place and see her again, soon, and take her out.

The boy Phil was sitting in a chair now with his thighs pressed together; he was holding the cat on his lap, stroking and fondling it, bent over and murmuring to it, and he was apparently still too young to know what a pansy-looking way that was to sit. When he looked up there were shadows under his eyes as plain as dust. He probably spent a lot of his time like this—indoors, hearing his mother's relentless talk and longing for it to stop, dying a little when the alcohol began to thicken her tongue—and Evan had to feel sorry for him. Well, but even so, if he didn't like this kind of afternoon, why didn't he go outside? Why didn't he get into stickball games in the street, or get into fights with Italian kids and learn a few things about life?

"How old are you, Phil?" Evan asked him.

"Fifteen."

"Oh? You look younger than that."

"Yeah, I know."

"You go to school around here?"

"Yeah, I go to—" Phil began, but his mother broke in and talked him quickly down.

"Oh, well, that doesn't matter any more," she explained, "because he's our wonderful big prep-school boy now. He'll be going to *prep* school in the fall; isn't that exciting?"

Evan said it was fine, and Charles mumbled something appropriate too; but then Charles had to blink a few times, looking around into various parts of the room. There was nothing about this place, or these people, to suggest the kind of money a preparatory school would probably cost. Whoever the absent father was, he must now be writing out an avalanche of other checks, on top of the alimony, paying for more and ever more unnecessary things.

". . . Well, it's a small school," Gloria Drake was saying, "and it's not as old as some of the better-known ones, but it has a certain character of its own. I think he'll have a marvelous time there, and I think it'll do him a world of good . . ."

When the man from West Village Motors came to the door, Evan left the building with him and took him down the street to have a look at the car. It didn't take long. A very few minutes later Evan was back in the Drakes' apartment, accepting more sherry, turning to face his father with a mixture of humor and apology as he reported that the man had told him the car would have to be towed away and scrapped. "He said to me 'This is junk you got here, pal. Nothing but junk.'"

"Oh!" Rachel Drake cried. "What a terrible thing for anyone to say about your *car.*" And she looked instantly shy because those were the first words she'd spoken to Evan.

"Oh, well, it's a very old car," he explained to her, not quite brave enough to meet her lovely eyes. "I should've known it was practically finished."

"Well, I think you're wonderful," she said, and she was consciously flirting with him now, "if you can take something as important as a car and just let it be destroyed, without any regrets."

"Some things you do are worth regretting," he told her; "others not." He could almost never express his thoughts as neatly as that, and it pleased him until he remembered it was something he'd heard his father say.

Phil Drake had looked openly astonished that his sister could say "I think you're wonderful" to a man she'd scarcely met. And Rachel seemed to know how her brother felt, because the two of them were now engaged in a little battle of looks, both of them pink in the face, each fearfully daring the other to make some punishing remark. They were clearly accustomed to a heavy dependence on each other, this brother and sister, and that seemed to confirm Evan's first impression of the Drakes: none of them would ever be strong.

But the girl was growing up fast. If you could get her away from this crappy little place, if you could bring her out into the nourishing sunlight and build her up and have her and keep her long enough, she might easily turn into a woman who'd be worth your blood, worth your life, worth everything. And if nothing else, she would be worth the try.

With Evan's help in the dialling, Charles called the eye clinic and cancelled his appointment; then he made a collect call to Cold Spring Harbor and told his wife they'd be a little late. And he'd scarcely turned away from the phone before still another heavy, brimming glass was pressed into his hand. This woman didn't know the meaning of surrender.

". . . Well, hasn't this been delightful?" she asked an hour later, when they were able to begin inching toward the door at last. "Oh, and wasn't it a funny way to meet? Just imagine: if your car hadn't broken down exactly where it did, and if you hadn't happened to ring our bell, out of all the other bells . . ."

Like shy conspirators, Evan and Rachel hung back a little from the others gathering at the doorway.

"Can I call you sometime?" he asked her very quietly, while Phil watched both of them with a partly lifted upper lip.

"Yes," she said. "Yes, I'd like that."

And no sooner had the door closed on their visitors than Rachel Drake began to feel like an exceptionally pretty girl. She felt almost like a girl in the movies, because meeting Evan Shepard had given her the opening episode of a movie she could play over and over in her mind whenever she felt like it. Her saying "I think you're wonderful" was the line that would let the audience know how bold a girl she could be, for all her shyness, and Evan's saying "Can I call you sometime?" was the one that would always mean their romance had now begun. It didn't even matter that all further episodes would have to wait until after his phone call, because this wasn't the kind of movie you'd want to rush through anyway.

Oh, but what if he didn't call? Every time she asked

herself that heart-stopping question she'd feel desolate for a while, but those spells didn't last very long. Soon her lungs would go back to work and she'd feel blood in her veins again, because she knew he would call; she was certain of it.

"Boy," her brother said. "Boy, Rachel, if this guy Evan doesn't call you up I guess you'll probably commit suicide, huh?"

"Oh, don't be boring," she told him.

"That sounded to me like a very silly thing to say, Philly," their mother said from across the room.

"Well, okay, I'm sorry," Phil said, and to make sure they'd both heard him he said it again: "I'm sorry."

Apologies were as common as blame in this small, fatherless family, and forgiveness was always in the air. Affection mattered. Until Phil was nearly eleven they had addressed one another in a ritualized baby talk that no outsider could probably have followed, and even now they often said "I love you." If any two of them were more than an hour late in getting home, the one who was at home alone and waiting would be sick with anxiety.

The Drakes had changed their place of residence twelve times in thirteen years. They'd been evicted twice, but it wasn't always the scrape of poverty that kept them moving: Gloria would often be impelled to find a new place only because the old one seemed alien to her nature in ways she seldom felt obliged to define. At certain disorderly intervals between one home and the next they had found they could only cling together like disaster victims, warding off a vast bewilderment with the laughter of artificial bravery or with groundless, pitiably tearful quarrels; then they'd settle uneasily into new surroundings and wait once again for a stirring of forces beyond their control.

All three of them had a weakness for the mirror that hung on the living-room wall of this current, temporary apartment; Rachel might have spent an hour there now, admiring the shape and tilt of her face at various angles, if she hadn't known her brother would be watching.

Instead it was Gloria who monopolized the mirror in the fading light of the day. She touched up her hair and tried several different facial expressions to suit the word "congenial," which had occurred to her as the perfect way to describe Charles Shepard. This glowing afternoon would be unforgettable, always, because Charles Shepard was the most congenial person she'd met in years.

"Oh, weren't they nice, though?" she asked her children. "I can't get over what a nice, congenial time we all had. And *I* think we'll be seeing more of them soon, don't you?"

Then her face froze with a frightening thought. "Oh, but I didn't—" she began, and she could see her rising fear reflected in the children's eyes. "I didn't talk too much, did I?"

"No, no," Phil told her. "No, you were fine."

The Shepards, father and son, did get a little looped at several Village bars that afternoon, taking pleasure in their wasted day and their newfound interest in each other, taking their time because the last train wouldn't leave for hours, and they laughed easily whenever either of them mentioned Gloria Drake or gave a little parody of the way she'd talked.

"I thought the girl seemed nice, though," Charles pointed out.

"Yeah," Evan said. "Oh, yeah; very nice."

"Very pretty girl, too."

"Yeah."

But Evan was afraid his father might now say "You going to take her out?" or something like that, and it was always important to keep matters of private business to yourself when you lived with your parents. Besides, he was ready to give another impersonation of Gloria Drake, and he didn't want to lose the momentum of the comedy.

"Hey, Dad?" he said. Then, stepping away from the bar, he tried to gather up and bunch the clothes on the left side of his chest to form a bulge there in the approximate shape of a woman's breast. With one hand he made conspicuous gestures of cupping and fondling what was meant to be the point of it, and in an effeminate voice he said "My, I was beginning to *worry.*"

"Well, that's—that's good, yes," Charles said after an appropriate chuckle. "Still, I think we've probably made enough fun of her now, don't you? As a matter of fact—" He swirled the ice in his drink, took a sip, and put it back on the bar. Then he stood straighter and settled the fit of his suit coat with several smart tugs at the hem of it, as if it were a military tunic. "As a matter of fact," he said again, "there's never been anything funny about a woman dying for love."

And Evan had to think that over, impressed with his father's insight, before he agreed that his father was probably right.

4

Evan found a bargain in a much-used, nine-year-old car a few days later; then he telephoned Rachel Drake for a carefully planned, oddly breathless little talk, and a day or two after that he was back at her door.

"Oh, hello," she said. "Come on in."

There was the reek of catshit again, and the grubby upholstery, and the torrentially talking mother—"Well, how nice to *see* you again, Evan; is your father well?"—and the frail, moody boy. But Rachel looked lovely in a fresh blue dress that she might have bought especially for this evening. Evan knew everything would be okay in a minute, if he could only get her out of here fast, and it was.

". . . Well, you certainly are a good driver," she told him far uptown as he headed for the George Washington

Bridge. "You're never nervous, are you. There's such—authority in everything you do. Everything you do with the car, I mean."

"Yeah, well, I've always liked to drive," he said.

He was planning to take her to a place he knew along the Palisades where you could walk out into a little field and have a spectacular view of Manhattan in the colors of the setting sun. Then they'd go to a certain restaurant he thought he'd be able to afford, on the outskirts of Teaneck, and what happened after that would depend on how well they were getting along.

With the car parked behind them at the roadside, he led her through tall grass and laurel shrubs until they came to a flat rock of the right height and size for sitting, and he laid down his folded jacket to protect the seat of her dress.

"Oh," she said when they were settled there together. "Oh, that's really something, isn't it."

"Well, I've always thought so, yes."

It was something, all right. The unimaginable skyline of New York, seen from this cliff across the Hudson, was more than enough to take your breath away. It let you know at once that all those yellow- and orange- and red-struck towers, with their numberless blazing windows, were there for better reasons than commerce; they were there for you, as if you'd wished them into being, and their higher purpose was to enhance your aspirations and accommodate your dreams.

Evan knew he could probably put his arm around her and kiss her now, but thought it might be better to wait. Instead he took hold of one pale, delicate hand on the rock, as gently as if it were a bird, and the funny thing was she pretended not to notice. Her dead-serious face remained in profile to him, fixed on the extravagant sight across the river, though a heavy blush had come into her neck and cheek. Shyness could be nice in a girl, but this one might have a tendency to take it a little too far. If he were to make a lunge and kiss her now, would she pretend not to notice that either? Well, damn; she probably would. And what if he were to run his hand up the inside of her leg?

"You're very shy, aren't you," he said.

"Yes, I am."

But at least she looked at him when she said that; she seemed to be examining his face as though she couldn't yet believe the perfection of it. Then it occurred to him that "Yes, I am" was a better and braver answer than if she'd said "No, I'm not," or "Depends what you mean by shy," so he kissed her quickly and lightly on the mouth.

"Okay," he said, getting to his feet, and he reached down to help her up. "Let's go."

It wasn't only Evan Shepard's face that Rachel found hard to believe; it was everything else about him. The broad-shouldered, meaty, graceful way he moved and turned was an unconscious performance that she thought she would never tire of watching. Some twenty-three-year-olds retained a boyish quality in their stance and bearing, and she guessed that could be attractive too, in its own style, but Evan always looked like a man.

And he knew so much! His unfailing poise, his easy flow of talk and his flawless handling of the car had only been overtures, and so had the neat surprise of his stolen kiss. She kept thinking about that kiss as he guided her down a suburban sidewalk and into what turned out to be an extremely nice, quiet restaurant: no other boy or man she'd met could have brought off a charming little kiss like that. If he'd held it a moment longer they might both have been too embarrassed for words, but he'd known just how to dart in, get it, and pull back again with the right kind of smile. And the best part was that now there would be no shyness at all when the time came, later tonight, for the real kissing to begin.

Seated across from him in this well-appointed place and waiting for further enchanting things about him to unfold, Rachel ordered a dry martini for the third time in her life. Evan's voice took on just the right blend of courtesy and command in addressing the waiter—that in itself was a fairly enchanting thing—then sometime later, over a dinner that proved remarkable for conversational ease on both sides of the table, he told her he'd been married and divorced and had a daughter of six.

She knew it would take a little while to sort out all the implications of that startling news. The very words "divorced" and "daughter" were too resonant of maturity to be absorbed right away.

"Where is she now?" she asked.

"My daughter?"

"Well, of course, her too; but I meant your wife. Your former wife."

"Oh, she'll be graduating from college this year, if I'm not mistaken," he said. "Or no, wait; I guess that was last year—but I don't really know what she plans to do next; her parents don't tell me much. It's her parents who look after the little girl, you see—they bring her over to the house sometimes, or I go over there—but they don't tell me much about Mary, and I don't ask questions."

So that was her name. A very young Long Island girl named Mary had fallen in love with Evan Shepard years ago, when he was very young too; there had been raptures of the flesh and of the spirit; she had given birth to his child, and now he didn't really know what she planned to do next.

"Is she pretty?"

"Who, Mary?" he said, and looked down at his plate. "Yeah; oh, yeah, she's very pretty."

On the way back to New York that night, riding silent in the car beside him, Rachel began to suspect that Evan Shepard could do anything he wanted with her. Her main constraint arose in a vision of her mother's anxious face, and in knowing her mother would be appalled if she were to "go too far," even with a man like this, let alone if she were ever to "go all the way" with him.

Rachel's mother had never been a reliable source of information about sex; her unspoken view seemed to be that nice people didn't find it necessary to discuss things like that. She could evade almost any question with her little shuddering laugh, or by saying there'd be plenty of time for Rachel to learn whatever she might need to know—and the troubling thing about this attitude was that it seemed always to come from carelessness, or laziness, rather than from any kind of principle. When Rachel was thirteen her mother had neglected even to tell her about menstruation until it was too late—until Rachel, at home alone on the day it began, had run bleeding and terrified to a stranger's apartment, where a kindly woman explained everything ("This just means you're a woman now, dear . . .") while a kindly man went around the corner to buy her a box of Kotex and a little pink elastic belt.

Even now, at nineteen, she felt heavily handicapped by ignorance. She could count nine boys or men who had taken her out alone on "dates," over spans of time that ranged from one or two evenings to half a year or more, and she knew there must be girls who wouldn't consider nine too meager a total (there were even retrospective moments when nine could be made to seem a pleasing abundance); still, some of the boys on her list had revealed by the way they used their hands, if not by the very way they breathed, that they were as heavily handicapped as she was; and a few of the men had made cold, smiling, frightening remarks that spoiled everything.

Not long ago a national weekly magazine had given surprisingly prominent space to an article on sexual relations before marriage. Rachel had started to read it with quicken-

ing interest, not even minding the author's overuse of
words like "realistic" and "sensible," but then her mother
came into the room and said "Oh, I wouldn't bother with
that if I were you, dear. They only publish those things to
be—you know—to be sensational." And when Rachel
looked around for the magazine the next day, wanting to
finish the article in privacy, she found that her mother had
thrown it away.

Was there really any reason, then, to be cautioned by
thoughts of her mother at a time like this? How could her
mother be hurt by what she wouldn't know and couldn't
find out?

Well, but even so—and there was no denying it—even so,
Rachel was afraid. The palms of her hands were moist in
her lap as Evan's car brought her back into the dark and
intricate swarm of Manhattan, and she was very much aware
of the pump of her heart. Maybe all virgins were afraid, or
maybe fear afflicted only those virgins who'd been tyran-
nized by their mothers; in any case, the worst part of it now
was that she couldn't imagine a respectable way of saying
no to Evan Shepard. He would laugh at her; he would think
her a child and a fool; he would dismiss her as if with a snap
of the fingers, and she'd never see him again.

But the remarkable thing, as they sat talking softly with
the car parked snug and silent at the curb near her house,
was that Evan didn't try to overwhelm her. He didn't even
make a pass at her breasts or her thighs—two moves she
had learned to fend off in fairly agreeable ways but would
probably have let him accomplish. All he wanted tonight, it
seemed, were kisses—long, embracing, Hollywood kisses
with open mouths and a sweet mingling of tongues. It was
almost as if he were saying Listen, I can wait for all the rest
of it, can't you? Oh, listen, I know an awful lot more about
this than you do, dear, and I know it's going to be better if
we take our time.

When he said goodnight to her in the vestibule at last, after waiting just long enough to make sure she'd found the door keys in her purse, she was faint and dizzy with hating to let him go.

"Will you call me?" she asked helplessly. "Will you call me again, Evan?"

"Well, of course I will," he said, looking back to smile at her in a way that would soon become habitual: a mixture of pity, fond teasing, and readiness for love.

On the road home to Cold Spring Harbor that night, knowing he'd made a good impression, Evan allowed himself to fool around with the idea of getting married again—but this time of having it come about in a better way, and for better reasons.

It wasn't until he was getting ready for bed, with a very few hours left before he'd have to be up for work, that a disconcerting question came into his mind: if he got married again, what about the mechanical engineering? Just before he fell asleep, though, it occurred to him that marriage and college wouldn't necessarily have to rule each other out. Ways could be found; arrangements could be made. When you were twenty-three and in command of your life, you could do anything.

5

Throughout the summer and into the fall of that year it became increasingly clear to Evan and Rachel, and to both their families, that they might as well consider themselves engaged.

Gloria Drake supposed it was all very nice, though it would certainly have been nicer if Evan had ever brought his father to the apartment again, but she felt unprepared and ill-equipped for this kind of thing. Most of the time she couldn't even believe her daughter was old enough to be in love; she still thought of Rachel as a little girl meticulously lining up half a dozen dolls for display on her bedroom floor, or breaking down in tears over matters as small as the denial of an ice-cream cone.

On nights when Gloria stayed up late enough to see

Rachel come dreamily home she was always unsettled by
the girl's appearance: clothes crushed and hair awry, eyes
dazed and mouth swollen, with the lipstick eaten away.
Love was often said to be torment, but Rachel could make it
seem like punishment as well.

Another thing: Gloria had come to suspect that Evan
wasn't entirely to be trusted—wasn't, perhaps, to be
trusted at all. There was a little too much of the devil in that
handsome face. Sometimes, as when he narrowed his spar-
kling eyes to give you a sidelong glance, he looked like the
kind of boy who might seduce and abandon a girl without a
moment's remorse.

"Rachel, I think we ought to have a talk," Gloria said one
afternoon in the living room, where Rachel had set up the
ironing board to press the pleats of a sexy-looking white
skirt she planned to wear that night. "I don't think Evan's
being very considerate of you in this long, aimless court-
ship. If you're engaged there ought to be a wedding date,
and it ought to be soon."

"Oh, mother." And Rachel looked up impatiently in the
steam of the electric iron. "Can't you see how unfair that
would be to Evan? He has a career to think about. He's
going to be an engineer, as I've told you and told you, and
he's going to need—"

"All right, but how long does engineering school take?"

"Well, it's four years, but the point is—"

"You want to be engaged for four *years*?"

"*No!* Will you please let me finish, mother? The point is,
a great many college students *are* married. We may be able
to get married after Evan's first or second year, because by
then I'll probably've been working long enough to build up
our savings. I'll have a steady job, you see."

"I don't like the sound of this," Gloria said decisively.
"When Evan comes over tonight I think the three of us had
better sit down, right here, and discuss it."

So that was what they did. The young couple sat listening together on the old sofa, holding hands, while Gloria spoke plainly. She pointed out that long engagements had always been considered unwise, for obvious reasons, and she urged them to be married not later than November. Otherwise, she said, it would be only sensible for them to "release one another from any promises."

When she'd delivered that speech she felt acquitted of her responsibility. She had taken the right line and chosen the right words. Meeting unexpected challenges as they arose, absorbing the jolt of each surprise and then making quick, firm decisions—this was the kind of activity she had come to think of, over the years, as living by her wits.

The young people sat conferring together in murmurs; then Rachel turned back to her mother and said they'd think it over, while Evan appeared to be preoccupied with a loose thread on his coatsleeve.

"Mrs. Drake?" said a deep masculine voice on the phone, a very few days later. "This is Charles Shepard." He happened to be in town this afternoon, he said, and he wondered if she might be able to meet him somewhere for a drink.

At the mirror she tried on three different dresses, none of them quite clean, and two ways of fixing her hair before deciding she was ready. She felt as thrilled as a girl, because it had been years since she'd gone out into the city alone to meet a man, and so she had to caution herself not to be ridiculous. She knew perfectly well Charles Shepard had called her only because he'd heard about her ultimatum; now he would want to present an opposing view. Well, she would hear him out, and then she would try to win him over. This would be still another occasion for needing to have her wits about her.

The place he'd specified was the high, wide, quietly throbbing lounge of the Pennsylvania Hotel, and it was in keeping with the style of this uncommonly congenial man to have chosen such a tasteful setting. He didn't seem to see her until she was within a few feet of his table; then he blinked, looked apologetic, rose to his full height like a military man and made a charming little bow. When they were settled she asked the waiter for a bourbon with a very small amount of water, and the roof of her mouth began to pucker pleasurably at the thought of it. This was going to be nice.

". . . So I thought we ought to discuss it thoroughly," he was saying, "because there may be aspects of it that do require a little—" But before he could finish that sentence one of his forearms tipped over a glass of ice water that flooded the table.

"Oh!" she cried.

"Oh, I'm terribly sorry. Here, let me try and—are you all right?"

"No, I'm fine. It startled me, is all."

The waiter was back, expertly blotting and wiping, murmuring assurances that no harm had been done, and when he was gone again Charles said, "It's my eyes, you see. I have very poor vision. Sometimes I go blundering into things like a blind man."

It was possible, then, that he couldn't see the crepey sections of her face and neck, couldn't see the grease stain left by a fallen slice of sausage on the bodice of this best of three dresses, couldn't guess her age, wouldn't have to wonder what to do about the open loneliness and longing in the way she would always look at him.

He was talking now in a voice as proud and steady as it must have been in the days when he'd commanded soldiers, explaining how important it was that Evan be "entirely free" to enroll as a full-time college student; and he said he was certain Rachel understood that too. Rachel had even told him as much, during one of the times Evan had brought her out to the house, and he hadn't been at all surprised to hear it: Rachel was far too intelligent a girl not to understand such a thing.

"Well, of course," Gloria said, meaning to agree only with the part about Rachel's intelligence, and now she could feel the whiskey beginning to do its subtle, wonderful work in her blood and brains. "And I can understand it, too, Mr. Shepard, but I'm afraid I—"

"Oh, no, please," he interrupted. "Call me Charles."

"Well, that's nice, Charles, and I'm Gloria. Still, I'm afraid I really can't see Rachel going to work as a typist or a waitress or something for what might turn out to be years, with no security beyond a vague plan of marriage at some future time. The point is there mustn't be any chance of her being hurt."

"How would there be any chance of that?"

She had to think it over for a minute, watching her empty glass being taken away and replaced with the gleaming fullness of another drink. Young Evan might occasionally strike her as a boy who could treat a girl lightly, or badly, but he was, after all, the son of this good and thoughtful man who wanted nothing but the best for both children. Even if his going to college did entail some element of risk for Rachel, well, life itself was a risk. Maybe you had to have a man's mind to think as straight and as clearly as that.

"Oh, well, I don't know, Charles," she said at last. "I suppose it's just that I still think of Rachel as a child."

"Well, that's—curious," he said, "because I think I'd describe her as a mature and responsible young woman."

And she could tell from his face and the texture of his voice that he knew he'd won the argument.

For another hour and more, using each other's first names a little more often than necessary, they talked and

drank as if their interest in each other were spontaneous—
as if they were friends—until suddenly it was past seven
o'clock. Charles had meant to be home by this time, but
now it seemed only courteous to ask Gloria Drake if she
would join him here for dinner. First, though, he said he
would have to make a phone call.

Waiting at a phone booth with a dollar bill in his hand
while an obliging bellhop placed the call for him ("There
you go, sir; oh, thank you, sir") Charles knew it was foolish
to be spending so much time and money in this place; still,
it couldn't be helped.

". . . Well, I've told you how the woman talks, dear," he
explained to Grace. "There isn't any way to stop her. But I
did accomplish the main thing: I got her to agree with us.
There won't be any more pressure on Evan now, and that's
a mercy, don't you think? . . . Right . . . Well, of course,
dear, and I'm sorry . . . Well, certainly. There's a can of
tuna fish on the bottom shelf of the right-hand cabinet over
the sink; then if you'd like to warm up some of the cream of
mushroom soup we had last night you'll find that in the
refrigerator, in the small pan, and you'll find some crackers
in the left-hand cabinet, up over the stove . . ."

As Gloria watched him coming slowly back toward the
table she thought she had never seen a man more—well,
more presentable. Cold Spring Harbor was well known as a
region of "old money"—large or modest family fortunes
husbanded through the generations—and the people there
couldn't have asked for a more appropriate representative
than Charles Shepard. You could tell his vision was poor
from the careful way he walked, but that seemed only to
enhance his dignity. He certainly didn't look as though he
might go blundering into things like a blind man; he looked
like the kind of man who might still, somehow, turn out to
be the hero in the story of her life.

"Oh, I wish you'd tell me more about Cold Spring Harbor, Charles," she said when he was seated across from her again. "Because do you know what I'd like to do someday? I'd really like to go out there and stay as long as I can, and discover it all for myself."

"Yes," he said. "Well, it's a very quiet area; really rather dull, in many ways . . ."

When Gloria got back to the apartment that night all her senses thrummed and sang with the pleasure of the evening. But she'd scarcely had time to fix herself a drink for bed when Rachel and Evan came in, hours earlier than usual, and the first thing she saw in their two sober faces was that Rachel looked triumphant. They had something to tell her.

"We've decided you're right," Rachel announced, holding fast to Evan's hand as they sat facing her again. "We're not going to wait any longer. We want to get married right away."

"Well, this is really—this is really very strange," Gloria said, "because I had dinner with Evan's father tonight, you see, at the Pennsylvania, and we came to agree on the other plan. The less definite plan."

"Oh," Rachel said. "Well, but then it isn't you and Evan's father who want to get married, is it. It's me and—it's Evan and me, isn't it."

Gloria didn't know what to think. She supposed it was good to see this kind of spirit in a child who had always seemed entirely too soft for the world; still, there was something unsatisfactory here that wouldn't quite come into focus.

And it was troubling too that Evan hadn't yet said a word. He had nodded and rumbled as though in agreement while Rachel presented their case; he had allowed his hand to be squeezed by one and then both of hers; but why didn't he speak up? Wasn't it supposed to be the man who did the talking on occasions like this?

"Well, Evan," she said, "I'm afraid your father's not going to think this is a good idea at all."

"Oh, well, I wouldn't worry about it, Mrs. Drake," he assured her in a sleepy voice. "He'll come around."

This young man might have seemed disturbingly devilish for months, but tonight, in contrast to Rachel's bright, proud face, he looked bland. He looked like a boy worn to fatigue and ready to give in, ready to submit to the stubborn terms of a girl holding out for marriage. Well, okay, what the hell, his weary eyes seemed to say; why not?

And only after making those assumptions about Evan was Gloria able to identify the unsatisfactory thing she had sensed in all this. Wouldn't it be a pity, really, for a girl to get married just for the sex of it?

"No, but really, Charles," she said on the phone a day or two later, "isn't it funny how we're letting them go ahead with the very thing you and I decided would be so—so illadvised?"

"Well, it's hardly a question of 'letting' them, is it," Charles said, sounding tired. "They're both old enough to do as they please, aren't they."

And she told him she knew that was true; still, for a long time after hanging up the phone, she could only sit on the sofa and try, unsuccessfully, to think.

She wished Phil were home, so the two of them could find a way to talk this whole thing over. Phil might still be only a boy, but there were times when the clarity in what he had to say could cut through a lot of confusion. And she wished he were home anyway, even if they weren't able to talk—even if all he wanted to do was fool around with the cat or examine his face in the mirror, even if he lapsed into the kind of willfully exasperating childishness that suggested he would always be younger than his age.

She missed him. His letters from the Irving School were long and sometimes funny enough to be read aloud, but they never concealed his unhappiness there. He probably wasn't sturdy enough for prep-school life. He was too sensitive; he had too much imagination for his own good; and in those ways he was like his mother.

Rachel was different. For all the softness and the crying over ice-cream cones, Rachel was the most stable member of the family: she took after her father.

Softness and stability—it might seem an odd combination, but Gloria knew how substantial a combination it could be. She understood too that a girl getting married just for the sex of it must be a common-enough mistake— girls had probably gotten married for that reason since the beginning of the world—but it was one mistake she'd never made.

She had been thirty years old, a veteran of several affairs and extremely anxious about her future, before agreeing to marry Curtis Drake. And she'd known all along that anxiety wasn't a very good reason for marriage; still, it had now begun to seem a better reason than this ignorant, virginal susceptibility of her daughter's.

Or was it possible that nobody's reasons could be all that clearly defined? Maybe men and women came together in ways as random and mindless as the mating of birds or pigs or insects, so that any talk of "reasons" would always be vain, always be self-deceiving and beside the point. Well, that would be one way of looking at it. Another way, even if it did require more piercing and poignant kinds of memory than she could bear to summon most of the time, would be to acknowledge that Curtis Drake had once won her heart.

"Oh, you say the nicest things," she could remember telling him, many times, and she had always meant it, though it wasn't easy now to sift out even the nicest of the things he'd said.

She had liked the trim shape of his head and the way he held it, and the set of his shoulders. She'd liked the depth and resonance of his speaking voice, too, in times of tenderness, even though she'd always known it could take on a harsh rasp in their quarrels, and that it could rise and thin out into an almost feminine whine on a line like "Gloria, can't you ever be reasonable?"

In the years since her divorce she had often remarked to other people that she couldn't imagine what had ever possessed her to marry Curtis Drake, but when she was alone she knew better: she could imagine what had possessed her. Certain old songs on the radio late at night, and especially one, could still make her cry for him:

> We could make believe
> I love you,
> Only make believe
> That you love me . . .

But she would have to put all that out of her mind now, for better or worse, because there were wedding preparations to attend to.

She had always fancied the Episcopal Church—everybody knew it was the only aristocratic faith in America—and so she was badly disappointed when a chilly rector told her on the phone that there couldn't be an Episcopalian wedding because of Evan's previous marriage. During the next few days, using the phone book as a source of reference, she drew up a short list of Presbyterian and Methodist churches that seemed worth looking into, but she couldn't take much interest in what she was doing. She'd grown fretful and bored with the whole problem when it was happily solved in an unexpected phone call from Charles Shepard.

There was, he said, a nondenominational chapel in Cold Spring Harbor that might provide a pleasant ceremony; then afterwards they could have a sort of small reception at the Shepards' house. Did that sound suitable?

"Oh, wonderful," she said. "Oh, that's perfect, Charles."

On the morning of her wedding, Rachel Drake was so tired and nervous she could barely pack her suitcase. She would have given anything to crawl back into bed and sleep for a few more hours, but that was out of the question.

"Mother?" she called through the open door to the living room. "Do you have the timetable out there?"

"The what?"

"You know; the train schedule. Because I can't remember whether it leaves at nine twenty-five or nine fifty-five, and I—"

"Well, dear, there's all the time in the world," Gloria called back. "We don't even have to be at Penn Station until almost eleven; then we can have a leisurely cup of—"

"No, no," Rachel said impatiently, "I'm taking the earlier train—didn't I tell you this?—I'll be going out with Daddy."

"Oh," Gloria said after a significant pause. "No, you didn't tell me that."

And Rachel chewed her lip in fear. Her mother's ungoverned displays of emotion were frightful, and this could easily develop into a bad one. "Well, I certainly thought I'd told you," she said. "I could've sworn I'd told you days and days ago. Anyway, it doesn't matter, does it? We'll all be together for the whaddyacallit, the wedding, and for the reception and everything."

Then her mother appeared in the doorway with the sad, ironic little smile of a tragic actress, wearing a splendid new dress that had cost almost a third of this month's check from Curtis Drake.

Gloria wasn't accustomed to keeping her temper when all other elements of an unfair situation cried out for her to lose it. Only a few times before in her life had she held everything back this way, managing to control herself, and she had soon forgotten, each time, how lofty and noble it could make her feel.

"Well, of course, Rachel," she said quietly. "I'll do whatever you wish."

There wasn't much sense of loftiness or nobility left by the time she rode alone on the later train that morning. She was preoccupied now with how awful her cheap old winter coat looked; she could only hope there would be some inconspicuous place to hang it, or dump it, before walking into the hush of the nondenominational chapel. ("Oh, there's her mother," people would whisper in their pews. "That's Rachel's mother. Doesn't she look nice?")

She knew Rachel would probably take care of introducing Curtis Drake to the Shepards, and to the Shepards' guests—surely that was how these things were done when the bride's parents were divorced—but she knew she wouldn't draw an easy breath until that part of the day was over and Curtis had gone home. And the very thought of him shaking hands with Charles Shepard made her wince—even made her squirm a little in her train seat—because Charles was a tall man and Curtis was five foot four.

"Well, of *course* we're the same height, Curtis," she'd told him crossly once, standing barefoot at the mirror of some forgotten bedroom, long ago. "Come and see. Come and look at us."

But when he complied, stepping up beside her in his socks with a bashful, self-conscious smile, she saw at once that she'd been mistaken: he was shorter. They must look utterly ridiculous together every time she wore high-heeled shoes, and other people must always have known it.

"Well, it's not really all that bad, dear," Curtis told her. "We're close enough. You can still say we're the same height, if that's how you'd like it to be."

Sitting straight and alert in the taxicab that took her away from the train, Gloria tried to see all she could of the subtle community sweeping past on either side. She knew she couldn't expect to see very much, because one important characteristic of the people here was their disdain for ostentation of any kind; still, there were a few quick, small rewards for her curiosity. Once she saw a blue-white pebble driveway, uncommonly clean and wide between two elegant stone pillars, but it vanished in a blur of hedges before she could even hope for a glimpse of the house it led up to; another time there was a sign reading Cold Spring Harbor Historical Society, and that was satisfying in itself.

The chapel was smaller than she'd imagined, but that didn't matter because there weren't very many wedding guests; everything, apparently, had been planned on a small and dignified scale. Charles Shepard sat only a few feet away, in a front-row pew across the aisle from her own, but she guessed he hadn't seen her come in. She guessed too that the thin, high-shouldered woman beside him was his wife.

Then an electric organ began to emit various slow, unsteady sounds. She supposed she should have known that Curtis Drake would want to "give the bride away," but it came as a little shock, even so, to see the two of them make their solemn way toward the altar. They were both too small even for small-scale pageantry, and their two embarrassed faces looked exactly alike.

Gloria had a cigarette in her lips and was ready to strike the match before she remembered you weren't supposed to smoke in church, which seemed a cruel deprivation. How long did these things generally last?

But soon enough she found herself smiling fixedly in the back seat of a car packed with strangers, heading for the Shepards' reception, and that meant the day might still be saved.

All her life, from the time she was eight or nine years old, Gloria had relied on a neat, nearly automatic little trick of her mind for adjusting to minor disappointments. When you opened the bright wrappings of some meager or poorly chosen gift, you simply let your mind tell you it was just what you wanted; that way you could always make the right response, and you could even believe it.

"Oh, isn't this nice," she said in the instant of her first, sharply disappointing look at the Shepards' house—small, ordinary, all made of brown-painted wood and too-closely flanked on both sides by bigger, better houses—and then she said it again, while getting out of the car, to make it true. "Isn't this a nice house."

Now there would be a party, and Charles Shepard might open his arms to greet her with a decorous kiss on the cheek.

But there weren't enough people in this place to make a reception. Except for a laughing cluster of guests around the bride and groom, near the liquor table, there was hardly anybody here at all—and Charles couldn't have opened his arms for her even if he'd meant to, because he was carrying a drink in each hand as he approached her across the empty floor.

"I'm afraid my wife won't be able to join us," he said. "She hasn't been feeling well; she's resting now, upstairs."

"Oh, well, I'm sorry," Gloria said. "Was she the lady sitting with you in the church? In the chapel?"

"No, that was my sister. She lives over in Riverhead. Curious: it's not really very far away, but this was the first time we'd seen each other in years."

"Has your family all come from around here, then? For generations?"

"Well, 'generations' makes it sound a little grand," he said, looking as embarrassed as if she'd inquired into their financial affairs, "but yes; on my father's side I suppose we do go back a ways. My mother was from Indiana, though; that sort of breaks the pattern; and my wife is from Boston."

"I'd really been looking forward to meeting her today; your wife, I mean."

"Yes, well, she'd have liked that too," he told her, "very much. But I'm sure there'll be other times soon. After all, we're all sort of related now, aren't we. We're a family."

That struck Gloria as a remarkably nice thing to say, and it warmed her as she watched him move away to another part of the room. But then she felt chilled again, all at once, because Curtis Drake was shyly bearing down on her.

"Well, Gloria," he said.

"Yes; well, hello."

This was awful. She knew she should probably have called him "Curtis" but there wasn't any way to make her tongue pronounce the name.

"Doesn't Rachel look lovely?" he said.

"She certainly does, yes."

"Oh, she's always been lovely, of course, but there's something about the way a girl looks on her wedding day that really brings it all home for you. Makes you very glad and very humble; very proud."

"Yes. Yes, I know."

Oh, this was horrible; and it might have gotten worse if Curtis hadn't raised his whiskey glass in a sad, casual salute and turned from her in search of someone else to talk to.

It wasn't until she was aboard a dirty, swaying, heavily rattling train for New York that Gloria realized she'd be going home to an empty place. Her daughter gone for good, her son away for many more months, she would now awaken to the hours of each new day alone, in silence, and never with anything to do.

6

For days after the Japanese attack on Pearl Harbor, Charles Shepard was almost sick with chagrin. He wasn't yet fifty; he knew the army would take him back if it weren't for his eyes. He made a careful trip to lower Manhattan for another, stronger pair of those well-publicized glasses; then he reported for an army physical, but he had no luck with the eye doctor. No luck at all.

It was several more days before he gave full attention to another line of thought that had been in the back of his mind all along: the army might never take him now unless things got bad enough for medical standards to be relaxed, but they would almost certainly take his son. Evan was healthy and smart and strong: he'd make an excellent soldier and would probably qualify for officers' training.

There'd be no chance of his getting overseas too late for *this* war; and so, as a lieutenant or even a young captain, he might serve to justify his father's life.

That was why Charles had begun to feel well again when he rode down the Island to Amityville for his first visit with Evan and Rachel in their new home, which turned out to be an oddly sumptuous apartment with peach-colored walls.

"So what are your plans, Evan?" he asked as soon as Rachel was out of earshot in the kitchen. "You going to enlist?"

"Well, I think so, yes. I'd certainly like to. The thing is, though, I think I'd better hold off on it a while now, until Rachel's a little more—settled. She's pregnant now, you see. We just found out this week."

"Oh. Well, I suppose that does sort of complicate things. Still, the army'd always provide for her and the baby, and very generously too."

"Oh, I know that, Dad."

"Well, I know you know it, of course. And I know you'll do whatever's best." But he had to acknowledge, in silence, that he was deeply disappointed. All the way down here, obliged to hire a taxicab because he could never again drive a car of his own, any more than he could ever command a company of men, he had believed there was every reason to expect better news.

"Coffee, gentlemen?" Rachel called, emerging from the kitchen with a tray of bright cups and saucers, and now it was time to prepare and deliver a nice little speech about how fine it was to learn she was having a baby.

". . . And then, of course, the other factor," Evan was telling him, "is that I might not have any say in the matter— if I get drafted, that is."

"Yes. Well, that'd be another story, wouldn't it." And Charles could feel his spirits beginning to lift again. It would be another story, but it might be almost as good: draftees could qualify for officers' training too.

It wasn't until he was on his way out that afternoon, shrugging into his overcoat as they walked him through room after peach-colored room to the front door, that Charles thought to ask what proved to be an awkward question.

"How much are you kids paying for this place?"

Evan hung his head in a dumb, cowardly way that Charles hadn't seen in years, but Rachel came through with the precise amount of the rent as brightly as though she didn't know it was going to make trouble.

"Oh," Charles said, taking in the dull shock of the information. "Well, that's a little—that's a little on the preposterous side, don't you think? Don't you think it's about three or four times as much as it ought to be, if you still have any plans for engineering school at all? This is foolishness, Evan."

Exasperation wasn't a very good note to strike at the end of a visit like this—Charles knew that—but he was determined to stand here waiting until his son looked him in the eyes like a man.

"Well, I think I can handle it, Dad," Evan said, and at least his head was up and facing in the right direction now. "And the thing is we like it here, you see. We both like it here a lot."

In March Evan's draft board summoned him for a physical examination.

Rachel tried to be brave about it because that was how young wives were shown to be in the movies, but she was perilously close to tears as she went about the poignant business of fixing his breakfast. She felt almost as if this were the day of his going into the army itself, or even the day he'd be sent overseas.

All he had to do today, though, was stand and walk buck naked in an echoing civilian gymnasium among hundreds of other bare-assed men, each with a set of numerals drawn in lipstick across his chest, each with his "personal effects" slung in a little cotton bag around his neck. It didn't take very long because the doctors all worked quickly, but there was time enough for Evan to find a surprising pleasure in the visions of soldiering that began to crowd his mind.

He felt sure he could withstand the rigors and embarrassments of basic training, which was often said to be the worst part; he knew he could learn to love the clean, oiled, weighted and balanced potency of his M-1 rifle, and now he could imagine wanting all the rest of it: helmet, field pack and cartridge belt, with the canteen hung against one buttock; canvas leggings strapped under the insteps of high-cut service shoes.

He could almost hear the boisterous talk and laughter of the barracks and the sharp, ringing count of cadence as his platoon moved out for the rifle range before sunrise—and he knew he would crave every chance he could get at rollicking nights in the bars and hotels of lost country towns with sweet, brassy little country girls.

There would be an ocean voyage in some comically overcrowded troopship; then there'd be a long ride and a long wait and a long hungry march on broken foreign roads to the front line; and so, soon enough, he would find out forever what "combat" meant; and he wanted that too.

"Shepard, Evan C.?"

He was singled out of his column of men, taken back, and made to submit to a second, more meticulous probing of his inner ears. When that was done the doctor sat down at a table, picked up half a salami sandwich in one hand and a fountain pen in the other, wrote "4-F" on a printed form, and took a greedy bite of the sandwich. He was evidently the kind of man who could write and talk at the same time, because while writing a sentence or two on the paper he explained everything, spilling crumbs of bread from his lips, before Evan could ask a question.

"Perforated eardrums," he said around his chewing. "And I wouldn't bother trying the navy or the Marine Corps; be better to save those people the trouble. Nobody's going to take you in with ears like this."

"Oh, thank God," Rachel said prayerfully when he came home with the news. "Oh, God, I'm so glad, and so relieved; aren't you?"

And he didn't know how to answer her (Well, maybe; maybe not; yes and no); so he didn't say anything. He opened a cold beer and sat down with it, knowing he'd need a little time and quiet to sort things out. It occurred to him, glancing around, that this ample apartment seemed to have shrunk. It had come to look and feel uncannily like the place in Huntington with Mary Donovan, years ago, except that it was costing him more than three times the rent.

"Aren't you going to call your father, darling?" Rachel asked. She'd been addressing him as "darling" since a week or two before they were married and he'd found it charming at first; lately, though, he'd begun to wonder if she wasn't overdoing it.

"Well, not right now," he said. "I'll call him in a while."

"All right. Oh, but I can't wait to tell my mother, and I want to call Daddy too." And she started swiftly for the telephone across the room.

"No, don't," he said, sharply enough to make her stop and turn back.

"Well, but they'll be so *pleased,* Evan."

"Look: just sit now, okay?" he told her. "Sit. Sit." And it

sounded like a command given to a nervous, well-trained dog, but she obeyed him.

If he'd ever spoken that way to Mary Donovan she might have put her hands on her hips and told him to go fuck himself; but then, that was the difference between youth and maturity. As a boy he'd had to contend with a proud and resentful girl; now, fully grown, he had earned the right to have a wife as placid as the wives of other men.

Well, but still, other men were saying goodbye to their wives all over the world. Other men were caught up in a profoundly hazardous adventure now, unable to guess how long it might last and not even caring. None of them were ready to die but they all knew their death was entirely possible; that was what would invigorate every waking moment of their lives.

And when they came back, these other men—or when most of them did—they would all have a decided advantage over Evan Shepard. They might look at him as if he were scarcely worth bothering with, the way the cops had looked at him the night he was booked for disorderly conduct. If they talked to him at all it would be in tones of condescension, rarely waiting to hear his replies. And whatever elaborate peaceful structures they might manage to build in the world, after the war, would always seem to be there for no other purpose than to shut him out.

One thing, therefore, was clear: they had better not find him like this. Evan Shepard was damned if they'd find him punching a factory time clock, fondling his thermos bottle of coffee and his little brown paper bag of lunch, doing mindless, underling things all day and then driving home in an absurdly cheap old car to this absurdly expensive place.

Something would have to be done, and soon; but first he would have to call his father.

Charles answered the phone in the kitchen while he was getting dinner started.

"Oh," he said. "Well, that's—that's really too bad, Evan. I can imagine how disappointed you are, and I'm sorry . . . Perforated eardrums; oh, yes. Well, that's always been a tough one. The medical assumption there, you see, is that you might be susceptible to many different minor infections, and it isn't worth the army's while to take responsibility for that kind of thing."

And for what other kinds of thing, dear God, had it ever been worth the army's while to take responsibility? What about a boy who couldn't believe the First World War was over? What about a girl who couldn't sleep in Fort Devens or Fort Dix, Fort Benning or Fort Meade?

Oh, Jesus, the army was a bitch and a slut and a whore. The army didn't care whether you loved it or not.

Charles was obliged to put the phone down for a minute —he had to turn over two sizzling pork chops on the grill and then to lower the heat under a frothing pan of peeled, boiling potatoes—and by the time he picked it up again he found he'd thought of a few encouraging things to say.

"Well, but look, Evan," he began. "There's a brighter side to all this. All the colleges are going to be a lot more accessible to you now, and for as long as the war goes on. They'll have to worry about keeping their enrollments up, you see, and I imagine they'll be very liberal with their scholarship programs and so on. If I were you I'd set my sights on engineering school right now, and I wouldn't let anything else interfere."

He'd gotten that far before remembering that Rachel was pregnant—maybe the news of pregnancy would always have to break over a man in wave after wave until it finally sank in—and so he had to wonder if all this college talk might now be pointless. A student with a crisp little working wife was one thing; what about a student with a wife and child?

But he took up the broken thread of his argument anyway, because he wasn't yet ready to let it go. "It seems to me the first thing you and Rachel ought to do is find a cheaper place to live; get out from under all that rent; then open a savings account and put away as much as you can every month, on a regular basis. I think you'll find it isn't really very hard to carry out a plan like this, Evan, if you're careful and if you never lose sight of your goal . . ."

Long before he'd finished talking, though, Charles had lost confidence in his own voice. He didn't like the bogus athletic-coach quality of it; he wasn't sure if a line like "Never lose sight of your goal" should be allowed to stand except as a ludicrous admonition in some comedy for children; he resented Rachel's pregnancy; and he was bitterly disappointed, in ways that got worse and worse the more he thought about it, by the perforated eardrums. Sometimes the world was just too fucking much.

He had washed the kitchen windows only yesterday, long and hard, and tonight one of their big black panes gave back a merciless reflection of himself: surprisingly old, surprisingly gaunt, looking forever as bewildered as he'd been in boyhood. He might have lingered at the window in a little ceremony of self-regard and self-loathing, but there were other things to be done. He had to mash the potatoes, drain the string beans, serve up the pork chops, and go tell Grace that dinner was ready.

He was almost as far as the sun porch when it occurred to him that Grace would probably say "Oh, God, how wonderful" or "Oh, that's marvelous" on hearing of Evan's draft classification, and he was right about that. She said both of those things.

Rachel's favorite radio program was a weekly series of half-hour Western dramas called *Death Valley Days*.

"Because I mean it really isn't just a bunch of cowboy stuff," she would explain. "They're very good, well-written little radio plays, and the acting's always very good too. I don't know how they can sustain such a high level of quality every week."

But *Death Valley Days* came on at seven o'clock, dinnertime for the young Shepards of Amityville, and that meant there could be no talk at all at their table as the two of them soberly fed themselves and listened to the little plastic Philco her father had given her for her sixteenth birthday.

It sounded like just a bunch of cowboy stuff to Evan, every time; still, it hadn't taken him very many weeks to decide he didn't mind. Anybody's marriage might benefit from an occasional embargo on talk. Besides, Rachel was a girl who depended on small, recurrent rituals—that was one of the things he'd come to know about her, and his very ability to identify so specific a trait made him proud of his own capacity for tenderness.

One evening in April, after a laconic, final exchange of cowboy dialogue and a significant whinnying of horses, Rachel turned off the radio without waiting for the theme music to come up at the end and said "Well, that wasn't exactly one of their better ones, was it."

She cleared away the dinner dishes, going about the job like an efficient young waitress, showing off a little to suggest how deft and graceful she could be. Then she brought her husband's coffee over to the sofa, in a softer lamplight, and sat beside him there with a cup for herself and a lighted cigarette that looked a little funny in her fingers because she hadn't yet quite learned to handle it. This was one of the hours Evan most looked forward to all day, every day, in the relentless drone and glare of the machine-tool factory.

"Darling, there's something I have to talk over with you,

because I promised I would," Rachel said. "But let's put it this way: if you don't care for the idea, we don't have to discuss it any further. We'll just forget it, okay?"

"Well, okay, but wait." He was looking at her with one of the long, fond, teasing smiles that were beginning to make her nervous. "You know what you do?" he asked her. "You say a lot of little things over and over, and always just the same."

"I do?" She looked troubled. "How do you mean?"

"Well, you say 'let's put it this way,' and you say 'don't care for the idea'—those are two examples, and I could probably come up with a whole lot of others."

"Oh," she said. "Well, I suppose that must be very—boring for you, then, isn't it."

"Oh, come on, sweetheart, I never said 'boring.' Whoever said 'boring'?" And he was afraid she might be taking this much too seriously, so he reached out to stroke or tousle her hair, but that didn't work because she'd just been to the hairdresser and didn't want to get it messed up.

"No, but still," she said after ducking and taking his hand away, "isn't that something everybody does? Develop certain habits of speech? You do it too."

"Nah, now wait a minute; that's silly. You're just—"

"Well, but it's true, Evan. You do. You always say 'a decided advantage'—never a 'distinct' or a 'definite' or a 'clear' advantage—oh, yes you do, and you say 'nah' instead of 'no' a lot of the time, and you always, always say—"

But by then it no longer mattered what either of them said, or was said to say, because any further talk was out of the question. With their cups and saucers safe on the coffee table and their cigarettes hastily stubbed out, the young Shepards of Amityville were in each other's arms.

At first the sofa seemed an adequate bed; then, with one foot, Evan shoved the coffee table far enough away to let

him help his writhing, gasping wife carefully down onto the
rug.

"Oh," she said. "Oh, Evan, don't stop."

"Oh, I won't, dear," he promised her, "you know that.
I'll never stop."

And it was clear to them both, in what little thought they
gave it, that the privacy of this big peach-colored place
would always be worth whatever it cost as long as it allowed
them an occasional chance to get laid on the floor.

It was an hour or more later, as they sat up in their bed
with two bottles of beer, before Rachel opened the topic
she'd said they would have to discuss. She told him there
was a house available in Cold Spring Harbor where they'd
have plenty of living space and even a separate room for the
baby, and where the rent would be less than a third of what
they were paying here; but there was a drawback.

"You're amazing, Rachel, you know that? How'd you find
out about this?"

"Wait—I'm getting to that. The drawback is, it wouldn't
exactly be private. It's a sharing arrangement, you see.
We'd be sharing the house with two other—two other people."

"Oh?" Evan frowned and began thoughtfully peeling the
paper label off his beer bottle. "Well, but still, that might
not necessarily be so bad. You know who the other people
are?"

"I'm getting to that. Just let me finish, okay?" And she
took a deep breath. "The point is, this whole thing is my
mother's idea. We'd be sharing the house with her, you see,
and with my brother, too, when he's home on vacations."

And Evan conveyed all his disappointment in one sad
syllable: "Oh."

"Well, I *said* I didn't think you'd like it, Evan, didn't I?
Haven't I made that clear from the start? We can simply
drop the whole subject now, if that's what you want to do."

But a minute later, as if the subject were still too whole and too fragile to be dropped, she said "I only wish—"

"Only wish what?"

"Oh, well, I was just going to say I wish I didn't have to call her tomorrow and tell her, that's all. She takes these things so hard. She'll be 'hurt.' She's dying to live in Cold Spring Harbor and she knows she could never afford to take this house alone, so she'll be 'hurt' for that reason; then the other thing is she's come to think of it all as some big generous way of doing *us* a favor, you see, so now she'll be 'hurt' for that reason too. She's impossible. I mean she's my mother and I love her and everything, but she's really a very, very—"

"Oh, I know, dear," Evan said quietly.

"God, and here I am talking about it when I said I wouldn't. Well, I'm sorry. I'm sorry."

"That's all right. I don't mind if you talk."

"She's really sort of—crazy, Evan. I mean that. She's always been crazy. Oh, I don't suppose anybody'd want to commit her to an insane asylum or anything, but she's crazy. All my life she's kept coming up with some scheme for a new place to live every year, and I think she always really *has* believed it'd make everything happier for us, each time. Isn't that crazy? Oh, and she used to say my father's a 'coward' because he hasn't gotten ahead in business; that's crazy too."

Rachel became slowly aware now, even while talking and listening to her own voice, that there might well be something universal about the pleasure a grown girl could take in disparaging her mother. Maybe it happened with sons and their fathers, too, or with all grown children and the ever-diminishing presence of parents in their lives; in any case, the knowledge didn't prevent her from pressing on, as if to see how far she would dare to go.

". . . And she doesn't smell very good, either."

"Doesn't what?"

"Smell very good. I guess that's a horrible thing to say about my own mother, but it's true. It may be that she doesn't take baths often enough, or that when she does take a bath she forgets to use the soap, but I've dreaded getting up close to her as long as I can remember. And do you know a funny thing, Evan? I've never told anybody about that until this very minute."

"Well, good," he said. "I like it when we tell each other things."

"She smells sort of like—rotten tomatoes," Rachel said in a hesitant, tentative way, distorting her face with the need to find a precise comparison, "or maybe more like old, rancid mayonnaise."

The pleasure of disparaging her mother was fading fast —maybe it would always be something you couldn't sustain very long—and besides, she wanted to go back and think about the completely unexpected remark her husband had just made: "I like it when we tell each other things."

Wasn't it supposed to be the girl, rather than the man, who said unashamedly vulnerable things like that? But the lingering expression of it was still there in Evan's eyes, and it was enough to make her tingle. She might even have tried to praise him for it, or to thank him in some way, if he hadn't spoken up first.

"How do you suppose your mother ever found this place?"

"Oh, probably from an ad in the paper: she always reads the real-estate section. She's spent her whole life reading the real-estate section."

"Seems funny, though, doesn't it, that a house of that size would be so reasonable? And furnished too?"

"Well, she did say the furniture isn't much, but she said it's 'tasteful' enough. Oh, and this is funny, Evan: she told me the house is 'very nicely located,' and I think all she means by that is that it's not far from where your parents live. Isn't it sort of—embarrassing, really, what a crush she has on your father?"

"Yeah, I guess it is."

"So anyway I've got the address written down, and the name of the rental agent, but I didn't really think you'd—"

"Well, it'd be worth looking into, wouldn't it?" Evan said. "And I mean Jesus—" He gave a brief, self-deprecating laugh. "Jesus, my *father'd* sure as hell like it, wouldn't he?"

The word "ramshackle" occurred to Rachel as they left the car and walked up to the house her mother's heart was set on: long, two stories high, white clapboard with a black tarpaper-shingled roof. It was similar to other cheaply built houses around the village, but its angularity was softened by a wealth of shrubs and trees; you couldn't quite see all of it at once.

"Plenty of space in there," the rental agent said, pocketing his bunch of keys, and he hung back to let the young people go first.

The interior walls had a makeshift look—big panels of light-gray insulation board that were framed and held in place by strips of wooden lath with all the hammered-in nail heads showing—but they were the same kind of walls that Evan's parents had in their house, so Rachel decided not to call attention to them.

And there was certainly plenty of space. The downstairs part of it alone looked roomy enough to accommodate four people, neither two of whom would necessarily have much to do with the other; and upstairs, that sense of strict mutual privacy became convincing.

Their bedroom, with the little adjacent room that would be the baby's, was practically an apartment in itself. There were generous windows along two sides of it, and there was a small fireplace that brought quick erotic visions into Rachel's mind. They could get laid here on the hearth rug by firelight, any time they happened to feel like it, with flames and shadows dramatizing every subtle movement of their flesh.

"I like the fireplace," she said to Evan, "don't you?"

"Yeah, well, it's a nice advantage."

"You mean a 'decided' advantage," she told him, prompting him to come up close and wink and give her a hug, while the rental agent looked discreetly away.

And Rachel would always remember it was that bedroom fireplace, with its ample little hearth rug, that won both of them over to her mother's plan.

7

By the end of Philip Drake's first year at the Irving School there was a hole the size of an apple in one elbow of his tweed jacket. He couldn't get it repaired because it was the only jacket he owned, and that small predicament seemed entirely in keeping with a greater hopelessness.

"Ah, Drake, you're hopeless," he'd been told, unnecessarily and many times, often just before being put through some crowd-pleasing humiliation that would turn out to be worse than the last. From the day of his talkative, overconfident arrival at Irving he had failed and failed at learning how not to behave like a jerk; and everybody knew what kind of life a jerk could expect in prep school. All through the fall and winter his hopelessness had been almost complete, and the worst of it was knowing he'd brought it on himself: he had "asked for it," as other boys were always quick to point out.

With the coming of spring there'd been surprising improvements: he began to attract less public ridicule and even managed to make two or three respectable friends. There was some basis for assuming things would be better next year (and "next year" would always hold a shining promise of renewal for every schoolboy), but first he would have to spend the whole of a summer at home—and "home," for Phil Drake, had now become as sketchy and treacherous an assignment as the dormitory he'd gone blundering into, talking and smiling, last September.

He wouldn't have minded going back to his mother's most recent apartment, the one on Hudson Street with the flaking walls and the doors that wouldn't quite shut, and with the good mirror where you could look for signs of maturity long overdue; it might not have been much, that place, but it was something he knew. All he could predict about Cold Spring Harbor was that his sister would be lost to him there—a married, pregnant woman—and that he would have to find some way of making peace with the taciturn, intimidating stranger she was married to.

After the sleek and quiet railroads of New England he found the rocking, clangoring Long Island train an insult to the nerves. He could hardly wait for the ride to be over, and so he was ready—standing in the aisle with his hauled-down suitcase in his hand, even before the conductor called "*Cold Sp'ng Harb'* "—or at least he was as ready as anyone could reasonably expect.

"Philly!" his mother cried, coming quickly across the living room of a long, oddly made house. "Oh, you look wonderful. Oh, let me feast my eyes on you."

She didn't usually want to feast her eyes on him until

she'd had a few drinks, and it must still be too early in the afternoon for that; or maybe, here in the country, she had taken to drinking all day.

"What's the matter with your coat, dear?"

"The matter with my what?"

"Your nice tweed jacket. It looks sort of all—slick."

"Well, it's very dirty, is the thing. When you've only got one of these you can never send it to the cleaners, you see, because you have to wear it every day."

"Turn around," she told him, and when she saw the hole in the sleeve she said "Oh, what a shame. Well, but listen: tell you what we'll do. We'll have it dry-cleaned right away, and we'll have some nice leather patches sewn onto the elbows. How would that be?"

And he could barely detect the weariness in his own voice when he said it would be fine.

"Rachel's dying to see you. She's upstairs in bed. Oh, it's nothing serious; just some little complication of pregnancy kind of thing, and the doctor wanted her to rest for a few days. So. Bring your bag, and I'll take you up to your room —oh, and I'm so hoping you'll like it, dear, because from the moment I saw that room I thought 'This is the place for Philly.' "

The staircase was walled in with the same insulation-board paneling that formed all the other walls; he guessed it must be part of some thrifty Long Island method of building.

"Well, this is fine," he said of his room. "I mean, really; it's very nice."

"Oh, I'm so glad," she said. "So glad you like it. See how big the closet is? Now come across the hall and see *my* room."

And once again, walking in and looking around, he assured her that everything was fine. Then she led him down to the other end of the hall, where they came to a closed door of paned glass that was tightly covered on the outside with a dotted-swiss curtain.

"Wait, though, dear," his mother said. "She may be sleeping. I'll check." She parted the curtain with one fore-finger, peeked inside, and said "Oh, good; she's awake." Then she knocked on one of the panes and called "Rachel? Your wonderful brother is home. Can he come in?"

"Well, of *course* he can."

And so he found his sister propped against pillows, put-ting aside what looked like a detective novel. She pulled up the bedclothes as if to hide her pregnancy but he got a glimpse of it anyway, unexpectedly big and heavy-looking under the flimsy stuff of her nightgown, when she raised her arms to give him a hug.

"Bring over that chair and come sit with me, Phil," she said. "Oh, it's been so long since I've *seen* you."

She wanted to know "all about" his year at school, and he gave her a brief, carefully edited summary of it, trying to imply that he'd had a pretty good time and concluding with an anecdote funny enough to make her laugh. Their mother lingered smiling in the open doorway for a little while, as though hoping to be included in their talk; then she went back downstairs.

". . . Oh, this is nothing," Rachel said of her illness. "It's just a dumb little bladder infection, but I think my doctor wants to keep me in bed until he collects a whole shelf of urine samples. First he gave me red pills, so the samples came out red; then he gave me blue pills, so the samples came out blue; and so on, and so on. I don't think he'll stop until he gets every color of the rainbow. No, but really, I'm fine. Never felt better in my life."

And that was easy to believe, from the look of her bright face. He noticed too that she'd changed this year: she looked older and prettier, in subtle ways, and he wondered if all girls were transformed like this when they started getting laid.

"Well, you've got a nice big room here," he said.

"Oh, yes."

He got up and took his chair back to the wall where it belonged. Then he said "My room's nice too. And I guess the house itself is kind of a bargain, isn't it. How d'you suppose she ever found it?"

"Oh, well." And Rachel gave him a quick, significant glance. "I think it probably helps if you've spent your whole life reading the real-estate section, don't you?"

Only rarely did the Drake children allow themselves a smile or a wink at their mother's expense—anything beyond that would have seemed a sacrilege—but they both suspected it would be a good thing if they could ever let themselves go. They might even be able, then, to talk about such matters as the way she smelled.

"No, but the main problem here is the dampness," Rachel was saying. "Have you noticed that? The whole house is damp. It wasn't something any of us noticed until after we'd moved in, but now there's no getting away from it. And Evan *hates* a damp house."

Back in his own room, unpacking his jumbled suitcase, Phil thought he could begin to notice the dampness—a faint tang of mildew in the air—but he didn't believe it was really the main problem here at all, and didn't believe his sister thought so either. The main problem, the thing about this house there was no getting away from, the part of the bargain that Evan Shepard must hate and hate, was having to live with Gloria Drake.

Because there was nothing else to do he went downstairs and sat around the living room for half an hour, first in one deep chair and then, to no purpose, in another. He supposed his mother was in the kitchen and hoped she'd stay there, even if it meant she would have more and more to drink. It wasn't easy to remember, now, that there'd been homesick times at Irving when he'd missed her as badly as if he were seven or eight years old.

The old cat came treading slowly in from the hall, and Phil said "Well, hey, there, Perkins; come on over here." He gathered up the cat and held it hanging in both hands as he eased himself far enough down into the chair to set his heels on the edge of the seat, as children sometimes do; then, bringing the cat's face in close, he kissed it on the nose.

That was when he looked up and found Evan Shepard standing in the room, watching him.

He spilled the cat instantly to the floor, got out of the chair as fast as he could, with a flailing of legs, and said "Oh, hi, Evan; just saying hello to my cat here, is all. How've you been?"

And even their handshake was a failure: Evan's hand closed so abruptly around Phil's that it clasped only the fingers instead of the palm; it must have felt as if he were shaking hands with a girl.

"Good to see you, Phil. How was your—how was your year?"

"Oh, it was okay, thanks."

And they stood looking each other over. It was the first time Phil had ever seen Evan in his factory clothes, shirt and pants of dark cotton twill, with an identification badge clipped to the left breast pocket, and that outfit made him want to apologize for attending a private school.

"Well, then," Evan said, with a nod to excuse himself, "see you later." And he went charging upstairs.

From the beginning, in this artificial household, dinner was the most oppressive event of the day. Rachel would place a small electric fan on the table before they sat down, because the weather was uncommonly hot and still for June, but the caged, buzzing, slowly turning face of it could only send faint new waves of warmth among the dishes.

"Oh, isn't this nice," Gloria often said at the brink of a dinner, and if Phil happened to glance at her then he could always see how afraid she was that tonight, once again, there might be no voices around the table except her own. Twice during the first week or so she made everyone's discomfort all the worse by saying, plaintively, "Well; I've always thought the dinner hour was for conversation." And not even her son could bring himself to look at her when she said that.

Evan Shepard hardly ever looked up from his plate, even in response to murmured questions from his wife, and his stolid concentration seemed to suggest that eating, no less than the day's work or than fathering children, was just another part of a man's job in the world. When he didn't need both hands for forking and cutting his meat, the muscular forearm of his free hand would always come to rest in the same way—canted up against the edge of the table, with the hand curled in a loose fist or holding a folded slice of bread, and Phil found that mannerism intriguing: it was the way working-class heroes ate in the movies. He tried to copy it a few times but it didn't come naturally and only made him self-conscious. One of the lesser things he had learned at Irving, without knowing he'd learned it, was that the prep-school style of eating involved one conspicuous elbow on the table and a tucking of your free hand down out of sight, hanging limp over your lap. That was the pose he kept reverting to now, involuntarily; it wasn't any wonder that many people seemed to think of prep school as a tucked-in, prissy way of life.

"Darling?" Rachel inquired—and it always startled Phil to hear her say that word as if it were her husband's name—

"Do you still like the salad, or should I try another kind of dressing?"

"No, it's good," Evan said with his mouth full, and with olive oil shining on his lips. "This is good." But he didn't look at her.

One evening their dinner hour was brief and free of its usual tension, if only because it held tensions of another kind: the elder Shepards had agreed at last, after several courteous postponements, to come over tonight for an after-dinner drink. Scarcely had the table been cleared and the dishes stacked before the doorbell rang; but when Gloria rushed to answer it she found Charles smiling there alone.

"I'm afraid my wife is a little tired," he said, "but she made me promise to bring her along another time; possibly some afternoon, if that's at all convenient."

"Well, of course," she told him, "as long as you'll—you know—as long as you'll keep your promise."

Out in the kitchen again, where she dropped two ice cubes on the floor in her nervousness, Gloria decided she didn't really mind Grace Shepard's staying away: having Charles here by himself would simply make it a different kind of evening, and one that called for a different plan. It was always important to have a plan in situations where you weren't entirely sure of yourself; otherwise your every chance at happiness could drift away and dissolve and be lost.

He was making small talk with the young people when she brought the liquor tray into the living room and set it with a little display of ceremony on the coffee table—or rather, he was allowing the young people to make small talk with him as he strolled the carpet and inspected things he probably couldn't see.

"Well, this is nice, Gloria," he said. "You've found a very comfortable house."

"Oh, well, it's damp," she said, letting him have the worst of the information at once to prove she wouldn't dream of withholding it. "That's the main problem. Still, we're hoping all this dry, warm weather'll make a difference. *I* think it will. What would everyone like?"

There was gin and whiskey; there was even a bottle of beer for Phil to nurse; and it wasn't long before their gathering seemed to glow with a sense of incipient pleasure.

"Charles?" Gloria said. "I'd almost begun to think we'd never see you again. Have you been avoiding us?" She knew that might sound like a tactless thing to say, or even a reckless thing, but it was a deliberate part of her plan. If you could go straight to the root of a social awkwardness and bring it out into the open, it nearly always worked to your advantage. The other person might feel momentarily embarrassed, but he'd appreciate your candor soon enough. The air would be cleared.

Charles assured her he'd been meaning to stop by for weeks—as, of course, had Grace; he said he couldn't imagine where the time had gone; he said he certainly hoped she hadn't thought he'd been rude.

And his embarrassment did seem only momentary: when the apologies were over he subsided in his chair and looked as though he felt better.

". . . Has Evan told you about what's happening at the plant, Charles?" Rachel inquired, and her sweet young face showed an earnest pride in being able to call her father-in-law by his first name.

He said Evan had indeed told him, and that it was excellent news; then the news itself was revealed in their discussion of it. Evan had been named as a likely candidate for the job of "parts-control supervisor," a responsibility to be taken along with his regular work as machinist; if it came through it would mean a pay raise substantial enough to bring the hope of engineering school a little closer.

And Gloria made appropriate murmurs of approval and congratulation, but her heart wasn't in it. "Parts-control supervisor" sounded as grindingly tedious as any other title Evan might bring home from the plant; and for that matter, even "mechanical engineer" seemed scarcely a term to put stars in a girl's eyes.

It wasn't easy to remember now that she had ever sensed the devil in Evan Shepard: as long as she'd known him here, in the close quarters of Cold Spring Harbor, he had impressed her only as a very, very dull young man. And that was always a source of dismay, because his father conveyed such an innate and unfailing elegance.

"You always look so *el*egant, Charles," she said. "That must be a brand-new summer suit, isn't it?"

"No," he told her, tugging the coat of it straight. "Matter of fact it's a very old summer suit; I've been wondering if I can make it last through one more summer."

"Well, it's certainly very—certainly very handsome. Very debonair." Then she brightened with a new thought. "Tell me something, Charles: are you always called 'Mr. Shepard,' or do people sometimes use your military title—sort of 'Colonel Shepard' or whatever it may have been."

"Oh, no, no," he said quickly. "I retired as a captain, you see, and that's not at all the kind of rank that carries over into civilian life."

"Oh, that's *mar*velous," she cried. " 'Captain Shepard.' I think that sounds extremely distinguished"—and here she turned happily to one and then the other of her children— "don't you?"

"Well, but no. Look," Charles told her, straining for patience. "Let me explain this if I can. If you ever meet a man in civilian life called 'Captain,' he's most likely to have been in the navy, don't you see? Rather than the army?

Because the naval rank of captain is far more—exalted: it's only one notch below a rear admiral; whereas the army's use of the same designation is an entirely different and lesser thing. I'm sure you'll understand."

It seemed to Charles that he hadn't heard this much of his own voice in weeks, or months, and he wasn't even sure he had yet made himself clear, though she'd responded with several little nods of comprehension as he talked. But now she said "Oh. Well, I don't care about any of that. *I'm* going to refer to you as 'Captain Shepard' anyway. Always." And she gave him a loose smile of lipstick and stained teeth.

There was probably nothing to be done about a woman like this. Dying for love might be pitiable, but it wasn't much different, finally, from any other kind of dying.

". . . Oh, and I'll never forget that wonderful afternoon on Hudson Street," she said an hour later as he hung smiling in the open doorway, all but dying to go home. "And wasn't it a funny way to meet? Just imagine: if your car hadn't happened to break down exactly where it did, and if you hadn't happened to ring our doorbell, among all those hundreds of other people's bells . . ."

Surprisingly, there were pleasant interludes in that big, damp living room—times of mutual trust that seemed to promise better times ahead.

"You're sixteen now, right, Phil?" Evan asked him once.

"Right."

"Well, then, you ought to have your driver's license. They teach you how to drive up there at whaddyacallit? At your school?"

"No, that's not the kind of thing they—no, they don't."

"Well, hell, it's easy enough to learn. Want to go out for a lesson on Saturday?"

"Sure," Phil said. "That'd be fine, Evan, if you have the time. I'd like that a lot."

On most other afternoons, when Evan got home from the plant, he would hurry upstairs to be secluded with his wife until dinnertime; but today he was having his whiskey with her down here in the living room—and the remarkable thing was that neither of them seemed to mind including Phil in the easy flow of their after-work talk. They even laughed together at one or two of Phil's jokes, as though Evan were just beginning to discover what a nice, bright kid he could be; and Phil could only hope they hadn't noticed the little spasms of shivering that repeatedly seized his shoulders and made him hug his arms as if he were chilled. None of this could probably have happened if Gloria hadn't been busy in the kitchen: it was her turn to cook dinner.

"It's a deal, then," Evan was saying. "We'll go out after lunch and we'll—or no, wait; damn. I'll have to be gone on Saturday."

And Rachel's face seemed to sag a little. This would be one of the alternate Saturdays when Evan left home for an all-day visit with his daughter.

"Well, we'll do it some other day, is all, Evan," Phil said, "and thanks. It's something I'd really like to do." If they could begin to do things together, almost as if they were friends, it might make all the difference; besides, there was a blood-quickening sense of adulthood in the very idea of knowing how to drive a car.

Evan squinted and frowned at his wristwatch; then he looked up again, apparently invigorated, and said "How about getting started right now? We've still got a couple hours of daylight; maybe more."

"Well sure, Evan, if you're not too—you know—not too tired or anything."

"Nah, nah, that's okay. Don't worry about it." Evan drank off the last of his bourbon and put his glass on the coffee table. "So. If you can pack up a couple of beers for us, dear, we'll be on our way. Or make it four beers, okay? Or make it six."

"Coming right up, sir," Rachel said as she hurried away to the kitchen; and Phil was glad to see her so pleased but wished she could have veiled it just a little. A subtler display of happiness might have been less embarrassing.

He and Evan were waiting at the front door, slumped in identical postures with their thumbs in their belts, when she came back with a heavy paper bag that clinked with bottles.

"Here you go, gentlemen," she said. "Have a good time."

But Gloria trailed her into the living room, looking even more bewildered than usual, and said "What's this?"

"A driving lesson," Rachel told her.

"Oh!" Holding her drink in one hand, she used the other to make a gesture of fear: the back of the wrist pressed to her brow, with the limp fingers splayed and hanging like a broken wing. "Oh, but you *will* be careful, Evan, won't you?"

"Careful of what?"

"Oh, well, I know I'm a foolish woman, but I'm terrified of cars. I've always been terrified of cars."

Phil was almost too ashamed to see what her gesturing hand was up to now, but he could predict it, and he looked anyway: she was cupping her left breast.

And it might have been nothing more than that—the mortification of his mother's carrying on—but from the moment he climbed into the passenger's side of Evan's car he was afraid he might fail at whatever test would have to be passed this afternoon. He felt a little better once they were out on the road; he'd found he could keep his spirits up by taking one greedy swig of beer after another, and Evan's agreeably calm demeanor at the wheel was reassuring too.

There was, Evan said, an almost deserted stretch of macadam some four or five miles from here; that would give them a good place to start. Then, opening a new topic, he asked how Phil felt about the way the war was going.

"Well, I haven't really kept up with the papers or anything," Phil said, "but I guess it's not so good, is it. Looks like it'll take a long time to win."

And Evan gave him a slightly mocking glance. "What makes you so sure we're going to win?"

"Oh, I didn't say I'm *sure,* Evan; I mean I guess it could go the other way; all I meant was—"

"Fucking right. Fucking right it could go the other way. And wouldn't that be something?"

This was the first time Phil had ever heard him say "fucking," though he probably said it often at work every day. Maybe he even said it to Rachel when they were alone, or maybe not; but then, what the hell did he say to Rachel when they were alone? And what, apart from "darling," did she say to him?

"Wouldn't that be something? Having Hitler in charge of everything? We'd be taking orders from the German army around the clock, and probably from the Japs as well. Can you imagine that?"

No, he couldn't. Phil Drake hadn't yet been able to imagine very much about the war; he couldn't even picture himself in the army, despite all the talk at school about an imminent lowering of the draft age to eighteen. It wouldn't happen to him for two more years, and nothing that far in the future was worth imagining now. Still, Evan Shepard's bleak vision of national defeat was disturbing—or would have been, if it hadn't prompted Phil to remember Evan Shepard's perforated eardrums; then he let himself relax a little in the car upholstery.

"Well, anyway," he said, "I guess I'll be lucky even to finish school before I'm taken in."

Phil Drake might not be much bigger or heavier at eighteen, but he'd be stronger and smarter and hardly ever silly any more. Except for a few widely scattered Irving School boys there would be nobody to remember what a jerk he'd been, and so the army might be the making of him; it might be the time of his life. Just before going overseas he would come home on furlough, wearing a uniform that could only make Evan Shepard weak with envy, and he'd say "Well, how're things going at the plant, Evan?"

Or, to be fair, Evan might have found his way into some second-rate engineering school by then, years older than any of his classmates, with Rachel at some menial daily work to make ends meet. But even a line like "How's college, Evan?" would be good enough, coming from a soldier in wartime. It would take care of the situation; it would do the job.

"This'll be as good a place as any," Evan said as he brought the car to a stop on a straight, empty blacktop road between a great many trees; then he got out and came walking solemnly around the hood.

Squirming and sliding over into the driver's seat as uneasily as if he knew he would never belong there, Phil made a frowning, nodding little show of attentiveness while his brother-in-law hunched close beside him to explain the gear shift.

"Keep the letter H in your mind," Evan said. "The gears are arranged in an H pattern, and it's very easy to remember once you've learned: it gets to be second nature. Watch, now. First; second; third; reverse. Got it?"

"Well, I think so," Phil said, "but I'll have to go over it a few more times. I mean it's not exactly second nature yet, if you see what I mean. Another thing: I don't quite get what it is the different gears do. The three forward gears, I mean."

"What they 'do'?"

"Well, I didn't say that right. What I mean is, I understand they provide three different degrees of power, but I don't quite—"

"Well, no; the power's in the engine, Phil," Evan said patiently.

"I know, I know; I mean of course I know the power's in the engine; all I meant was, they provide for the transmission of power in three different—"

"No, the transmission is what turns the rear axle."

"Yeah. Well, look, I don't think I'm really as dumb about this as I may seem, Evan; I'm probably only asking a lot of questions because I'm nervous, is all."

And Evan gave him a quizzical look. "What're you nervous about?"

Later, when the car was carefully set in motion with Phil at the controls, things only got worse. ". . . No, easy; easy on the *clutch*," Evan had to tell him, more than once, because Phil's trembling left foot kept working the pedal heavily and in spastic haste. Then the car did accelerate nicely for a few hundred feet, and he felt the thrill of its gathering speed until Evan said "Jesus!" and wrested the wheel from him with one quick, strong hand—just in time, as it turned out, to keep them from veering into a roadside ditch that looked about four feet deep.

Another time, when Phil was trying again to find the knack of letting the clutch in and out, they lurched and stalled dead in an embarrassing smell of gasoline.

"You flooded it," Evan told him.

"I what?"

"You flooded the fucking carburetor."

That was how the lesson went until darkness began to fall —nothing really taught; nothing really learned—and when Evan drove them silently home he appeared to be sulking, as though he'd been offended by the afternoon. It was clear now that there would be no further driving lessons unless Rachel could find some agreeable way of encouraging them; it seemed too, from the set of Evan's handsome profile, that he might now be thinking of ways to let her know, tonight, what a hopeless fucking idiot her brother was.

And Phil knew there might not be much profit or future in hating your brother-in-law, but that didn't mean you couldn't figure him out and see him plain. This dumb bastard would never get into college. This ignorant, inarticulate, car-driving son of a bitch would never even be promoted to a halfway decent job. This asshole was going to spend the rest of his life on the factory floor with all the other slobs, and it would serve him right. Fuck him.

"Well, hi!" Rachel called, looking up from the sofa as they came in, and her lips were shaped for saying "How'd it go?" but instead she said nothing. For years, ever since she'd been ten or eleven, her face had taken on this troubled, frightened look whenever there might be reason to dread an unfortunate report of Phil's performance in the outside world.

Gloria was sitting across from her, hunched in the middle of a reminiscent anecdote and talking steadily. She didn't even seem to notice that Evan and Phil were home—she had apparently forgotten her fears of violent wreckage on the road—and she didn't seem aware that Rachel was no longer listening to her.

Then it was dinnertime. When Rachel had plugged in the electric fan she plugged in her radio, too, and placed it on the table. They were just in time, she announced, for *Death Valley Days*.

"For what, dear?" Gloria asked.

"*Death Valley Days*. It's my favorite program. And they have a different story every week, you see, so it's not like a serial. If you happen to miss a few weeks, that doesn't spoil your enjoyment of it the next time."

And nothing, clearly, was going to spoil Rachel's enjoyment of it tonight. Absorbed in the opening lines of radio dialogue, she tucked into her meat and potatoes with the look of a girl determinedly at peace.

Beneath the cowboys' amiable voices you could hear their boots clumping along a hollow wooden sidewalk; then came an unexpected pistol shot. There were several masculine calls of command, one of them delivered in falsetto, and soon, with the music rising to suggest dramatic tension, there was a thundering of horses out across the great desert plain.

Gloria's face was terrible with weakness and reproach as she brought a wrinkled paper napkin to her mouth and blotted it in two or three places. She seemed to be trying several different ways of sitting in her chair, as if no position were comfortable or even secure. Then she wiped a few damp strands of hair from her forehead, lifted her chin to make herself heard above the cowboy sounds, and said "Well; personally, I've always thought the dinner hour was for conversation."

8

On some days, with Evan gone at work, the house seemed to be steeped in idleness. Almost any activity, any way of stirring up the air in new directions, was worth considering.

"*I* know what let's do," Gloria cried as she and Rachel were clearing away the lunch dishes. "Let's go to the movies."

And Phil could see at once that Rachel wasn't sure if she cared for the idea. As a mature young woman, thoroughly familiar with sexual intercourse and other intimate matters of that kind, could she really be expected to take part in an afternoon at the movies with her mother and her little brother? Still, she was visibly tempted; she was thinking it over.

"Well," she said at last, "all right—if you're sure we'll be back before Evan gets home. I don't want him ever coming home to an empty place."

"Oh, that's silly, dear. There's all the time in the world, if you'll just give me a minute to change my clothes. Do you want to change too?"

Rachel said she guessed she did, and it took longer than a minute; soon, though, their party of three was ready to set out, on foot, for the village. This was like old times.

When the Drake family went to the movies, wherever they happened to be living, they never bothered to find out what time the main feature began: much of their pleasure came from waiting for a prolonged confusion to clarify itself on the screen. Eventually, after various tantalizing elements of plot had gained more and more coherence either in development or in resolution, each of the Drakes would try to be the first to turn and whisper "This is where we came in"; then, more often than not, they would agree to stay through the end again, in order to intensify the story they already knew.

The movies were wonderful because they took you out of yourself, and at the same time they gave you a sense of being whole. Things of the world might serve to remind you at every turn that your life was snarled and perilously incomplete, that terror would never be far from possession of your heart, but those perceptions would nearly always vanish, if only for a little while, in the cool and nicely scented darkness of any movie house, anywhere. And for Phil Drake, the light-dappled shadows of this particular movie were especially sweet: he could sense the hushed presence of his mother here and his sister there, where they belonged. Oh, it might only be further proof of how young he was for his age and of what a wretched year he'd had at school, but these two women were still the people who mattered most to him.

It was probably better to go to the movies at night, when nothing much but sleep was expected of you afterwards; going in the daytime always meant you had to come out into the blinding streets of reality and find some way to face whatever was left of the afternoon. Even so, the Drakes liked to take a little time to let a movie clear itself out of their minds—they didn't want to lose the comforts of artifice any sooner than necessary—and they would often walk together in silence for a hundred yards or more before one or another of them broke the fading spell by speaking.

"Well," Gloria said. "That was nice, wasn't it."

"Oh, it certainly was," Rachel said. "And it would have been perfect if Evan could've come too."

"Well, I don't know, though," Phil said. "I sort of liked having it be just the three of us again."

But his sister turned on him crossly. "What an unpleasant thing to say," she told him. "Would you begrudge Evan a movie?"

"Oh, come on," he said. "Jesus, 'begrudge.' Why do you always want to talk that funny way?"

And the two of them might have gone on cutting and bruising each other all the way home that day if a tall boy on a bicycle hadn't pulled up at the curb, shaded his eyes from the sun with one arm and waved the other in an extravagant greeting.

"Hey! Phil Drake!"

It was Gerard "Flash" Ferris, one of the more dismal social outcasts of the Irving School, and he looked as pleased as if his fortunes had just taken a surprising turn for the better.

". . . Well, how *nice*," Gloria said when the introductions were over. "And what a coincidence, isn't it? Finding another Irving boy here, of all places? Does your family live here, Flash?"

"My grandmother does, yes ma'am. Out a little ways off Route Nine."

"Are you just visiting, then? Or will you be here all summer?"

"No, I'll be here. I mean I live with my grandmother, you see."

"Wonderful. Then you and Phil can have someone to—" and she almost said "to play with," but caught herself in time. "Someone to sort of kick around with," she said instead, uncertainly, as though she could only hope a phrase like that might be acceptable in adolescent usage.

Watching them talk, Phil felt he could almost read his mother's mind. Certain things about Flash Ferris—the good manners, the flawlessly tasteful sports clothes, the expensive bicycle—suggested at once that his people had money; and here in Cold Spring Harbor it might easily turn out to be the kind of "old money" that figured so importantly in her yearnings.

". . . Well, we'll certainly have to keep in touch, then, Flash," she was saying.

"Oh, we will," he promised her, and he tucked the Drakes' phone number carefully into his shirt pocket before he took a courteous leave of them and pedaled away.

"What a nice boy!" Gloria said when the family was walking again, and Phil decided he had better acquaint her with a few facts.

"Listen," he began. "Can you listen a minute, please? That kid's a—that kid's really a—I don't want anything to do with that kid. He's a jerk."

Gloria stopped on the sidewalk and gave her son the withering look she reserved for times when he'd let her down badly. "Oh, I might have known you'd make some silly trouble," she said. "You're a very strange, selfish boy."

"Will you listen a minute? Ferris is so hopeless he doesn't even care who knows it. This whole dopey thing of calling him 'Flash' got started as a joke, you see, because he's so slow and clumsy and he's always falling down, but then he decided he liked it; now he wants everybody in the world to call him 'Flash.' "

Gloria had made a little show of patience and self-control while waiting her turn to speak again, and now she was ready to make the most of it. *"You* listen, Phil. If we have an opportunity to meet a few congenial people out here, I'm not going to let you spoil it for the rest of us. You'd better keep that in mind." Then she started walking again, and Rachel went along with her.

"And another thing," he called after them, hurrying to catch up. "Another thing: I know he's very tall and he's got this very deep voice and everything, but you know what he is? He's fourteen years old."

"Oh?" Gloria said. "Well, I don't see how that necessarily makes any difference at all."

And Phil could only plod along beside her in silence, with his head down. He had always been able to recognize the gathering of an impossible situation.

There was the rare succulence of corn on the cob for dinner that night, which provided enough earnest, two-handed munching to spare anyone's being expected to talk; even so, it wasn't long before Gloria managed a few conversation-opening remarks.

"Well, we met a boy from Phil's school in the village today, Evan," she began.

"Mm?" Evan said without looking up. "Well, good."

"He lives near here with his grandmother and he seems very nice, but Phil says we're not supposed to like him at all. Phil's developing into a very strict judge of other people, you see. He has no mercy. I think the only person in the world he approves of these days is himself."

"Oh, Mother, *please,* " Rachel said. "Let him eat his corn in peace."

That was the first sign Phil had that Rachel wasn't mad at him any more; still, a line like "Let him eat his corn in peace" was scarcely any better, in its way, than what she'd said about begrudging Evan a movie.

And the awkwardness of it was plain to Gloria as she rose regally from the table to clear away her own unfinished dinner plate: just before reaching the kitchen door she said, with quiet scorn, "Ha. 'Let him eat his corn in peace.' "

When the phone rang a day or two later Gloria sprang to pick it up, and Phil listened to her half of the talk with mounting apprehension.

". . . Who? Well, I'm afraid I don't—oh, you're Flash Ferris's *grand*mother. Oh, well, how very nice of you to call, Mrs. Talmage. . . . Well, that sounds delightful, and of course we'd love to. I wonder if you could give me a few directions, though, so we can find our way to your—oh, good." Then she got busy with a pencil, writing things down, and Phil knew there would now be no escape.

The following afternoon, carefully dressed for tea, he and his mother were a mile from home, walking along the edge of a major highway, and as one sun-brilliant car after another swept past it left a swirl of tan dust that stung their eyes and seeped into their clothing.

"You sure we're going the right way?" he asked fretfully.

"Of course I'm sure. It can't be much farther now."

"Can I take a look at those directions you wrote down?"

"Well, I don't want to stop and go through my purse now, dear; besides, I think we're almost there. Watch for a sign that says Delco Batteries; that's where we turn left."

For the first time, then, it occurred to him that Mrs. Talmage had probably assumed they'd be coming by car. "Oh, Jesus," he said, "were those *driving* instructions she gave you?"

"Well, I suppose so, yes, but that doesn't matter. It's a very small community."

"Jesus," he said again. "Oh, shit."

"I think you know how I feel about that word, Philly."

"Oh, yeah? I thought the one you didn't like was 'fuck.' "

"Oh, *please*," she cried, and her hand made a move for her breast but didn't quite connect. "*Please* don't start being this way. You're just going to ruin a nice time."

"Yeah, yeah. 'Nice.' "

But a moment later all the trouble vanished from his mother's face. "Oh, look!" she said, touching his arm. "See up ahead? 'Delco Batteries'!"

There were acres and acres of Mrs. Talmage's property: wide rolling lawns in a perfect state of maintenance, with evergreens in the distance. Her handsome old house, probably her ancestral home, stood at the end of a well-raked pebble driveway that met your heels in unexpectedly buoyant, invigorating clicks and crunches.

"Isn't this beautiful?" Gloria asked her son in a near-whisper of reverence, as if they were in church.

In her shaded sitting room, waiting for her guests to arrive, Harriet Talmage had just discovered once again that it could be almost impossible—almost maddening—to have even the smallest kind of talk with her daughter Jane.

"Well, you certainly needn't feel *obliged* to stay, dear," she said, "if you'd rather get an early start back to town; I just thought it might be a pleasant afternoon. The boy is a school friend of Gerard's, you see, and Gerard says the mother is a very nice person too."

"I don't get it, though," Jane said. "Does this kid have to go everyplace with his mother? How come?"

That brought a mild snort of amusement from Warren Cox, Jane's "friend," who sat close beside her in the deep chintz couch. He was a plain bald man of forty-five or so, and his business suit was the color of chocolate ice cream.

"As a matter of fact," Harriet explained, "it was Gerard who suggested I ask the mother to come along. He felt it might be a nice gesture, and I agreed with him. She's new here, she may not know many people, and so on. Actually, Gerard is very mature and very thoughtful in matters of courtesy and consideration for others, as you may have noticed."

"Well, no," Jane said. "Can't say I've noticed anything like that. You noticed anything like that, Warren?"

"Nope," Warren Cox reported, "not yet, but I've sure as hell noticed how tall he is. Taller'n me, and he's got bigger hands."

The talk subsided then, but Harriet felt she couldn't relax until one of her daughter's thighs stopped rolling lazily in its hip socket, away from the other thigh and back, away and back. Having to watch the indolent slattern's roll of that leg was like having to hear Jane say "I don't get it" and "this kid" and "how come": it was enough to make your molars ache.

Harriet had long been resigned to knowing there were many things she would never understand. She wouldn't live long enough to make sense of the coarseness and vulgarity that had come to blight every decent impulse in the world today, and she would die without hope of finding any explanation of her daughter's life. Three stunted, broken marriages, an only child left here as an infant for Harriet herself to raise, and now this bewildering parade of "friends"— what kind of life was that, dear God, for a girl who'd started out with every advantage?

"Oh, isn't she marvelous, Harriet?" John Talmage had said many times, long ago. "Isn't she stunning? Isn't she a lovely girl?"

So it was probably a blessing, in a way, that John hadn't

lived to see the woman his daughter had become. He wouldn't have known what to make of her either, if only because she wasn't even pretty any more. She was too thin and sharp-faced and sarcastic as she nestled here with Warren Cox—and Warren Cox, God knew, was no prize: a commercial person, a sales person, the kind of man who said things like "*x* number of dollars." At lunch today, laboriously trying to explain some business procedure, he had said "*x* number of dollars" three times.

But now it was time for Harriet Talmage to rise from her chair and say "*So* glad," because the maid had just shown the visitors into the room. "I'm *so* glad to see you both. This is my daughter Mrs. Ferris, and her friend Mr. Cox—and I don't know *where* Gerard is, but I'm sure he'll be joining us shortly. Won't you sit down?"

When Flash Ferris did join them, very tall and sincere in his school clothes, it seemed to Phil Drake that the only thing to do was let the rest of the afternoon have its way with him: get through it, write it off, pretend it hadn't happened.

". . . So how's your vacation been so far, Phil?" Flash inquired when they were settled at a low, brightly laden tea table.

"Oh, not bad."

"You got a bike?"

"No, I don't."

"How come?"

"Whaddya mean, how come? I don't have one, is all."

Flash reached out to gather up two or three very small, neatly made watercress sandwiches. "Well, I don't know what I'd do here in the summertime without a bike," he said. "I ride every day. I know all the roads and all the towns. I've never liked being stuck in one place, is the thing."

And Phil was able to agree that he didn't much like that

either; then, for something else to say, he added that he'd been looking around for some kind of summer job.

"Well, good," Flash said. "Good luck with it."

". . . Oh, but perhaps you *know* them," Gloria Drake was saying to Mrs. Talmage over her carefully held saucer and teacup, on the other side of the table. "Captain and Mrs. Charles Shepard? Well, they're delightful people; I know you'd like them. And their son, you see, is married to my daughter; that's sort of what brought us all together out here. Captain Shepard comes from an old north shore family, though I believe his wife is originally from Boston. And actually, *I'm* the only real outsider: I was born and raised in Illinois, but I've considered myself a New Yorker for so many years now that I think I've learned to feel at home almost anywhere, as long as I'm among congenial friends. . . ."

Mrs. Talmage seemed able to take it all in with a fixed, pleasant social smile; but Mrs. Ferris was chewing with her mouth open and staring at Gloria Drake in the way a rude child will sometimes stare at a cripple. And Mr. Cox, snug beside her in the sofa, appeared to be ready for an afternoon nap.

As if resolved to begin his summer of artificial friendship without further delay, Flash Ferris got Phil away from the tea table as soon as politeness would permit and led him quickly upstairs, saying "Show you my room."

And Phil had to admit it wasn't really uncomfortable to sit around that well-appointed room trading pleasantries and little jokes: predictably enough, Ferris could act like a fairly decent kid when he wasn't in school. The trouble was that if this kind of thing were allowed to go on it could only make for serious embarrassment later, when school began again in the fall. Ferris was just the kind who'd know how to impose on an accidental summer's courtesy, and how to exploit it.

But then he made a shy announcement. "I'm not going back to Irving next year."

"You're not? Why?"

"Because I've been accepted at Deerfield, and it's a whole lot better school; that's why."

"Well, that'll be good," Phil said with a great sense of relief. "You can make a new start."

"Yeah." And the slight flicker of hurt in Flash's face showed at once that he understood the implications of a new start having to be made. "Well, I did make a lot of dumb mistakes at Irving, that's true," he said. "Still, I think I'll do better now."

"Sure you will."

Flash was up and slowly pacing the floor, holding his shoulders unnaturally straight and square, almost visibly practicing the way he would carry himself at Deerfield. He stood looking out a window for a while, as if the infinite possibilities of Deerfield could be glimpsed from here; then he turned back and said "Want to go down for some pimple juice?"

"Some what?"

"Pineapple juice," he explained, smiling, and for the first time that day he looked as goofy as his old self. "I call it pimple juice."

"You would."

There was nothing for Phil to do now but follow his host along a hall past a number of other rooms, then down a back staircase and outdoors onto a wide concrete area meant for the turning and parking of automobiles. On the far side of it was a row of garage doors that looked almost as long as the house itself; at closer range, a big ruddy man in shirtsleeves stood washing down a limousine with water from a garden hose.

"Well, Flash," the man said, cocking back the visor of his

chauffeur's cap, and his heavy face came open in an unpleasant smile. "And how are you today?"

"Hi, Ralph," Flash said guardedly, and seemed to hurry a
little.

"Still beating your meat, Flash?" the man asked him.
"Still pulling your pudding?"

"Don't pay any attention," Flash said to his guest.

"So who's your friend, Flash?" the man inquired. "Is he
your asshole buddy? Huh? Or does he take it in the
mouth?"

And the two of them had to walk across the whole ex-
panse of wet concrete before they came to a door that
opened into an enormous kitchen.

A girl who couldn't have been more than nineteen was
working alone in there, very trim in an off-white house-
maid's uniform, rinsing vegetables at a sink.

"Hi, Amy," Flash said.

"Hi."

She didn't look up, but Phil recognized her as the maid
who had answered his mother's ring at the heavy front door
today, and who had then brought the tea things into the
sitting room. Flash was busy at a great refrigerator, getting
out ice cubes and a half-gallon can of Dole; by the time he'd
filled two tinkling highball glasses and set them on the
kitchen table, the girl had left her work and gone gracefully
out across the parking area for a private talk with Ralph,
who looked pleased to see her coming.

". . . You don't want to pay any attention to that guy,"
Flash was saying. "He's nothing. He's just a big, dumb,
Polish son of a bitch. Oh, he's smart enough to know I'll
never tell my grandmother on him for the way he talks—
he's got *that* much intelligence—but in every other way he's
dumb as shit. All he knows is how to drive a fucking car."

As Phil took small, sweet sips of a drink he didn't want he
kept looking out the window at the maid and the chauffeur

and wondering about them. Surely the man was too old to be her boyfriend—he looked about fifty—but maybe he took a fatherly interest in her: maybe she had come to rely on his plain, straightforward advice in meeting the various uncertainties of her young life.

In any case, they were just concluding their conference when the boys walked out across the parking area again, a few minutes later. The girl was laughing behind her hand at something Ralph had said; then she turned from him and started back to her job.

"See ya then, Amy," he called after her, and he let her get twelve or fifteen feet away before he brought the hose around and gave it a little snake-like flip that sent a dollop of water splashing at her ankles.

"Oh, *Ralph,*" she cried, breaking into a run for the kitchen door—and when this particular girl ran, in that cream-colored skirt, her rhythmically churning buttocks were marvelous to watch. Phil Drake had made a firm, sensible decision not to think too much about girls this summer—it would be better to wait until his glands could catch up with his mind, or until his mind could catch up with his glands—but at moments like this he knew what a futile decision it was. If he didn't start finding out a few things about girls, soon, he was going to go crazy.

"Well, Amy's kind of a good kid," Ralph confided as he put the hose back to work on the sudsy, dripping limousine. "Or at least she *coulda* been a good kid; it may be too late now for any man to straighten her out. Know what her trouble is?" And he turned his smile on both the boys, who were dumbly waiting for the answer. "She finger-fucks herself too much. Simple as that."

Mrs. Ferris and Mr. Cox were gone from the sitting room —back to New York where they'd come from, or upstairs getting ready to go back as quickly as possible—and Phil found ample evidence that his mother had talked her heart and lungs and brains away all afternoon: there was a sad, telltale display of cigarette ashes on the oriental rug beside her chair, and she looked very tired.

"Well, you must come again, Mrs. Drake," Mrs. Talmage was saying. "It's been so nice."

"I'll give you a call tomorrow, then, Phil," Flash Ferris said. "Okay?"

"Okay."

And all the way home, or at least until the serious walking began, Phil knew he would have to agree with his mother that they'd both had a lovely time.

". . . No, but it's really too bad you don't have a bike," Flash pointed out, straddling his own bike at the curbside. "When do you think you might get one?"

"I've told you," Phil said as he slouched against a lamp-post, hoping to look like the picture of a normal, healthy local youth at ease. "If I get a job this summer I guess I could save up for one; meanwhile I can't afford it, that's all."

They were hanging around the skimpy village with nothing much to say and nothing to do. This was the second or third day of the easy companionship Flash had planned, and it wasn't developing very well.

There was a new picture at the movie house, so they settled for that as a way of killing a couple of hours; but they both seemed to know it would only leave them feeling jaded and edgy afterwards, when they came out into the sun again, and it did.

". . . Well, okay, so I'll see you," Flash called over his shoulder, just before rising on his pedals to pump his way out to Route Nine; and watching him go, Phil wondered ironically if it might be only in keeping with the rest of this lousy summer to find himself dumped by Flash Ferris.

But the next time they got together Flash was tense and brimming with a fine idea. Ed's Cycle Repair, in Huntington, had a nice, thoroughly rebuilt bike for sale at twenty-five dollars. How did that sound?

"Too much money," Phil said, and Flash looked at him as if he must be kidding. There weren't supposed to be situations like this in prep-school circles.

"You can't raise twenty-five *dollars?*"

"No; that's what I'm trying to tell you. I can't."

"Well, but couldn't your mother help you out until you—"

"No, she couldn't. She can't."

The incredulity was lessening in Flash's face—he seemed to allow that there might indeed be a few charity boys at a place like Irving, though he wouldn't have expected any of them to live in a place like Cold Spring Harbor—and he said "Well, okay. I know what we can do. I'll ask my grandmother to buy it."

"No, that's out," Phil said emphatically. "That's out. I don't want you doing anything like that."

"Why?"

"Because it wouldn't be right, that's why. I wouldn't feel right about something like that." And Phil could dimly hear, in his own voice, a tone of righteous, stubborn pride that he guessed he must have learned from movies about the Depression.

"Ah, come on, Drake, don't be dumb about this," Flash said, and that won the argument.

A day or two later Phil took a sluggish local bus into Huntington, where he met Flash at Ed's Cycle Repair, and there it stood—substantial and shining, bought and paid for. It wasn't quite the first bike he had ever ridden, though it might have looked as if it were from the way he wobbled out into the Huntington streets, but it was the first one he had ever owned.

"How you doing?" Flash called back to him, sailing easily ahead.

"Good. Fine." But as he hunched over the handlebars Phil had to acknowledge that this was still another example of how young he was for his age: straining to keep up with a fourteen-year-old, beginning to like the feel of a bicycle when everybody knew that boys and even girls of sixteen were expected to be driving cars.

Flash Ferris did seem to know all the roads and all the towns. During the next week or two they traveled west to Oyster Bay and east beyond Huntington to Greenlawn and Kings Park, and they rode away from the shore to a few inland towns as well. Phil had to admit he was having a pretty good time, if only because he hardly ever had to be at home, and he liked to discover how bright and inviting all these other parts of Long Island could seem.

"Well, I've made a decision about next year," Flash said one afternoon when they'd stopped to rest at a grassy little strip of beach along the shore road. He was sitting in the sand with his legs drawn up at ungainly angles, looking even gawkier than usual. "In January, once I've turned fifteen, I'm gonna lie about my age and see if the Marines'll take me."

There hadn't been many chances lately to give Flash Ferris the kind of disdainful response he'd always drawn at Irving, but this was a good one and Phil made the most of it. He was reclining on his elbows, squinting out across the water, and he let a few moments of silence gather before he turned to Flash's vulnerable face.

"Bullshit," he said. "That's about the silliest God damn thing I ever heard."

"Whaddya mean?" And Flash was instantly on the defensive. "I'm tall; I'm pretty strong; I might even pass for seventeen right now, except that waiting till January'll give me a chance to fill out a little more. Besides, the Marine Corps is loaded with kids who've lied about their age. Don't you read the papers?"

"You didn't get this out of the papers, dummy; you got it outa the fucking movies. And you'd never pass for seventeen. You wouldn't even pass for *fif*teen."

"Wanna bet? Wanna bet I don't look as old as you, or older?"

That brought the discussion around in an unwelcome way, and Phil didn't have a very good answer ready. "Ah, you're dreaming, Ferris," he said. "You're dreaming, that's all."

"Well, so what if I am?" Flash inquired, logically enough. "It's still worth a try, isn't it? So I'm gonna try for it, is all, and I don't see what's so funny about that."

"Yeah, yeah, yeah; okay."

It wasn't hard to erase that small unpleasantness before the day's bicycle riding was over: there were times when all you had to do was smile at Flash Ferris to make him blush and smile gratefully back. Then, a few days later, Phil had an important announcement of his own to make.

"Got a job this morning," he said as they sat together at a Huntington lunch counter, drinking fountain Cokes. "Start work tonight."

"Yeah? What kind of a job?"

"Parking-lot attendant at Costello's, out on Route Nine."

"You know how to drive?"

"No; but you don't have to move any cars on this job— you're not even supposed to, from what the manager told me. What you do is, when the cars come in you use a flashlight to guide them into the right parking space; then when people are ready to leave you guide them back to their car. Takes a little planning, because you have to keep the whole pattern of the lot organized so nobody's car ever gets blocked in or anything, but I think I can handle it. The house only gives me a token payment of five bucks a week, but the guy said I can expect to make thirty a week in tips; maybe more.''

Flash was clearly troubled as he stirred his crushed ice with a paper straw. "So can you still come out for rides?''

"Well, maybe once in a while, late in the afternoon, but the point is I won't be getting off work until four in the morning, you see; then I'll have to get my sleep. And it'll be seven nights a week.''

"Yeah," Flash said. "Well, but what'd you do this for, anyway? Take this job?''

"For the money; what else? And I need money for a whole lot of reasons.''

"Such as?''

"Jesus, Ferris, don't give me 'such as.' If you weren't rich you'd never say 'such as.' ''

"I'm *not* rich.''

"Oh, Christ, don't make me laugh.'' And Phil tried for a look of patient scorn as he got up and stepped away from the counter. "Come on, then," he said. "If you're finished with that, let's get going.''

There could probably have been no cleaner a way to arrange the necessary break with Flash Ferris, and the best part of it came at a little after five o'clock that afternoon, when they were riding home along Route Nine and approaching an intersection that made a shortcut to Phil's house.

"Guess I'd better peel off here and go on home, Flash," he called into the wind. "Gotta eat and go to work. So listen: take it easy, okay?''

9

A high, handsome electric sign—"Costello's"—brought people into an ample old bar and restaurant built out on pilings over the softly lapping water of the Sound. It was a nice-enough place, a little vulgar for some tastes but pulsing with romantic possibilities of its own kind. Nobody ever seemed to get bored there.

Hardly any of the regular employees paid attention to Phil Drake—they all knew he was only the summer kid who looked after the cars—but two or three of the waitresses would say hello to him when they showed up for work, and there was a hefty, slope-shouldered young busboy named Aaron who sometimes stopped to exchange a few words in the gathering dusk.

"So how's it going, Phil?"

"Oh, not bad, thanks, Aaron; how about you?"

"Can't complain. Staying out of trouble, anyway."

"Good."

And if ways could be found of making a grave and courteous little ceremony out of opening and closing car doors, Phil did his best to find them every night. In the long hours after dark he used his flashlight with conspicuous skill, but the tips were disappointing at first: many people didn't tip him at all, and he'd ride home in the morning with a loose pocketful of quarters and dimes that were hardly worth counting. Then one day he rode into Huntington and turned over a great deal of merchandise in a drab little army and navy store until he found what he was looking for: a chauffeur's cap of dark gray twill with a patent-leather visor, similar to the more expensive-looking cap of Ralph's uniform. That made a difference. He wore it low and square on his forehead, to show he meant business, and his tips picked up. At the end of the second week he folded a five and two ten-dollar bills into a gracefully worded little letter of thanks, addressed the envelope to Mrs. Talmage and dropped it into the mail with a nice, grown-up sense of knowing how to do things right.

It might not be much of a job, this parking lot, but it was the first job he'd ever had and he took it as seriously as the circumstances allowed. And it seemed to impress his sister, in what little he saw of her these days.

"I think it's wonderful that you're doing so well for yourself, Philly," she told him once. "We all do."

He did the "planning" part of it well enough so that nobody's car ever got blocked in and there were no other troubles, even with drunks, but there were unsettling moments.

For all the excellence and wisdom of his decision not to think too much about girls, it was shaken a few times every night. Most of the arriving customers were scarcely worth his attention; but he could never tell, at any hour from dusk until well after midnight, when he might be surprised by a pretty girl. A car would ease into its appointed spot, the dim glow of its ceiling light would come on inside and there she would be, combing her hair or freshening her lipstick. Then she'd squirm around and shift her weight, careful to keep her knees together as she slipped out of the passenger's side while he held the flashlight steady to help her find her footing. The man coming around from the driver's side to claim her would often be a soldier wearing the summer uniform of starched tan cotton, but with surprising frequency he'd be a civilian—sometimes even a civilian who didn't look very much older than Phil himself.

As they moved away toward the bright steps of Costello's the girls would hold their escorts by the waist or the arm or not at all—Phil decided there was no real significance in those three styles—and they didn't seem to walk across the lot so much as drift across it, their pale dresses floating and swaying in and out of shadows as if time were the last thing on their minds. Keeping a careful distance, he would sometimes follow a couple and try to overhear what the girl was saying: whole personalities of girls might be deduced from that kind of eavesdropping, but for the most part he heard only tantalizing fragments.

". . . Well, but we'll only have one drink here, okay? And then let's go right on home."

". . . Hasn't it ever occurred to you that I might be a little tired of hearing about what Linda likes and doesn't like? And how Linda feels? And what Linda has to say about this and that and everything else . . . ?"

Late one night he led a soldier and a lovely girl from the bar into the darkness, and the girl's voice was as sweet as a song. She was trying to reassure the soldier about something, though the words were indistinct at first until she said "But you're not insensitive, Marvin. You're *won*derfully sensitive."

And Phil knew he wouldn't hear anything prettier than that all summer. It stayed with him for hours as he needlessly patrolled the parking lot or stood looking through a chain link fence at the slick pilings and the black, gentle water.

"You're *won*derfully sensitive." It was exactly the kind of thing a girl might say to Phil Drake when he was old enough to deserve it—and it could even happen in two more years, when he'd be in the army and when all other elements of his life would be under control.

He often wished he could follow people into Costello's and find out what it was like at the peak of business hours—all he was ever allowed to see was the way it looked in the late afternoons, when guys in shirtsleeves were still taking upside-down chairs off the tops of tables, and the way it looked at the end of the night when they'd be putting the chairs back up again. He knew, though, that there were deep leatherette booths along three walls of the room, and he guessed that those were where most of the girls would probably choose to settle. Toying with their gin rickeys or their rum-and-Cokes in the throb and moan of the jukebox, they might let their free hands fall delicately onto the thighs of their men. And he knew he wouldn't forget certain popular songs of that summer of 1942 as they were wafted dimly out to him among the parked cars.

This was one:

> Missed the Saturday dance
> Heard they crowded the floor
> Couldn't bear it without you
> Don't get around much any more. . . .

And this was another:

Altho' some people say he's just a crazy guy,
To me he means a million other things
For he's the one who taught this happy heart
    of mine to fly;
He wears a pair of silver wings. . . .

I'm so full of pride when we go walking
Ev'ry time he's home on leave
He with those wings on his tunic
Me with my heart on my sleeve. . . .

When closing time came around he would stuff the flashlight in his pocket and walk through the service entrance into the kitchen—this was his only privilege on the job—and ask for a cup of black coffee.

"How come you always want black coffee?" a haggard dishwasher asked him after the first few nights.

"I like it black, is all," Phil explained, but the explanation didn't ring true: he knew he drank coffee black because that was how his mother drank it ("It's wonderful, Philly; it's very stimulating; it really perks up your spirits; this is the way the French drink it all the time").

"Want any ice cream?" the dishwasher asked him. "We got five flavors."

"No thanks."

"Piece a pie?"

"No, that's okay. Thanks anyway."

"Know something, kid? You're gonna rot your guts out, taking in all that caffeine without any nourishment." And the man shook his head in mild exasperation. "You're a sad case."

Sipping and wincing at his hot cup, Phil knew the old guy was probably right but didn't know what to say or do about it, and that made him feel even skinnier than usual.

Then Aaron the busboy burst through the swinging doors from the restaurant, whipping off his apron and dropping it into a laundry hamper. He made straight for a tub of maple walnut, mashed three scoops of it into an ice-cream dish and wolfed it down in what looked like no more than six or seven motions of his spoon. Then he lobbed the spoon and the empty dish into a sinkful of hot water and suds and turned away to take off for home.

"Goodnight, Aaron," one of the girls called, and then others took it up: "Goodnight, Aaron" . . . "Goodnight, Aaron" . . .

"So long, girls," he called back. "See you tomorrow."

And Phil Drake felt like a very sad case indeed as he pedaled slowly home along Route Nine.

But in the shrunken daylight hours, with money in his pocket and his firm tires whirring over asphalt and concrete, it never took him long to feel much better. He could go shopping now, even for things he didn't need. In the well-fanned depths of an old-fashioned hardware store one day he bought a jackknife for no better reason than that he liked the weighted feel of it in his hand; then later, closer to home, he made another stop and picked up a cellophane package of six Milky Way bars because Rachel had often said it was her favorite kind of candy.

"Well, how sweet, Phil," she said. "And how thoughtful. You remembered." But she said she'd rather not eat one of them now, if he didn't mind; she'd rather put them all in the refrigerator until they were nice and cold. "And I bet you didn't even buy anything for yourself, did you."

"I sure did," he told her. "I made a major purchase. Look."

"Oh, nice," she said. "That looks like a beauty. I'm afraid I can't open the blades, though, with these long fingernails. Will you do the honors, dear?"

And when he'd thumbed open both blades of the thing, a

long one and a short one, she said "Wonderful. Those two are all you'll ever want with this kind of knife. If there were any other things in it, like all the stuff in a scout knife, they'd only get in the way and spoil the balance of it, right? This kind of knife is exactly what you want for mumblety-peg and things like that—looks better and feels better too."

"Well, I guess so, yeah," he said, taking it back from her. "Hadn't really thought of that, though."

"You were the best mumblety-peg player in the neighborhood when you were about eleven. I could hardly ever beat you at that, or at any other target kind of game."

"Well, it's okay with me if you want to remember it that way," he told her. "What I mostly remember is that we never really played mumblety-peg at all, beyond learning a few of the hand positions. What we did was *play* at playing it. That's what we did with all the games, and with sports too; or at least I did."

"You did not, Phil," she said. "You really played. You certainly played touch football, when we lived in Morristown, and I'd come out and watch you almost every afternoon."

"Rachel, will you cut this out? Touch football is about the worst example you could've thought of. I *played* at playing it, that's all, and all the other kids were on to me."

But she was so serious now, insisting on her own spunky memories, that in the end he let her have whatever she seemed to need. Rachel had never been much of a companion in certain kinds of reminiscence.

When Evan got home that afternoon it was almost time for Phil to go upstairs and wash up for the parking lot, though not quite; he hadn't yet made his escape when his sister said "Phil? Have you shown Evan your knife?"

And so, like a bashful little boy, he had no choice but to offer up the jackknife for his brother-in-law's inspection and approval.

"Mm," Evan said. "Yes, that's a nice one."

All Phil had to do now was get out of this room, but he hadn't made the first two or three of the stairs when he was stopped by overhearing a little snort of disbelief or amusement as Evan said "Is he really sixteen?"

"Well, of course he is," Rachel said impatiently.

"I'll be God damned," Evan told her. "When I was that age I was out getting laid."

"*Ev*an!" she said.

Phil went through his washing-up as calmly as if he'd already decided not to give Evan's remark a moment's thought, not to let it get him down at all; but he had to hesitate a long time over whether to wear the chauffeur's cap on his way down and back through the living room again. He settled on the compromise of stuffing the cloth part of it into one hip pocket, with only the patent-leather crescent of the visor hanging free for ridicule—or for showing how little he cared about ridicule of any kind. That was how he left the house and covered the distance to the driveway, where his bike stood propped on its kickstand; and it wasn't until an hour later, speaking aloud to the chain link fence over the Sound, that he heard himself say "Yeah, well, fuck you Shepard. Just wait and see, you son of a bitch. You won't be laughing at me a hell of a lot longer."

10

"Darling?" Rachel Shepard inquired. "Will you be having breakfast here today? Or would you rather have it out?"

"Have it out, I think," Evan said. "That's simpler."

It was another of the Saturdays when he would go to visit his daughter, and Rachel never quite knew how to behave on these mornings. If she tried being bright and cheerful she was afraid of seeming *too* bright, *too* cheerful; still, giving any hint of the loneliness and jealousy she would feel all day might only be a worse mistake. She was as shy of meeting her husband's eyes as if he were a man she had just met; and later, along with the helplessness she felt when the front door closed behind him, there was always an unexpected sense of relief.

Mary Donovan's parents had moved down toward the south shore four years ago, so that Mr. Donovan could be closer to his job at Grumman Aircraft, and it couldn't be denied that they'd grown a little less cordial in their dealings with Evan Shepard. This new house of theirs was dominated by a heavily screened front porch, and lately—it happened again this morning—they managed to avoid any real greeting of Evan at all. At the moment he took a step or two up the concrete path from the sidewalk, the screen door opened just enough to let Kathleen out, all dressed up and all eagerness, all arms and legs and flying hair as she came running to meet him—"Daddy!"—and he dropped to his haunches and gathered her up in a hug. Then, when he looked up at the house again, there was a slow wave of a white-sleeved arm in the shadows behind the screen, like the curve of a fish near the surface of murky water. He couldn't even tell whether it was Mr. or Mrs. Donovan who waved, but the meaning of the signal was clear: a simple acknowledgment of shared responsibility.

"Well, don't you look pretty," Evan said. "Is that a new dress?"

"Yes. Mom bought it in New York."

"Good."

He had heard other fathers say that seven was "a nice age for a girl," and now he could easily see what they meant. From a distance Kathleen might look frail and disorganized, but up close, in his arms, there was a reassuring strength in her that suggested a healthy young heart. And girls of seven did seem to like their fathers with an unqualified enthusiasm; that was another nice thing.

"So what would you like to do today?" he asked as he set her carefully down on the pavement and took her hand for walking. "We can do whatever you want."

"Oh, it doesn't matter," she said. "Let's decide later, okay?"

When they were settled in the car he reviewed several possibilities. "Well, we could drive along the south shore a little ways and see the big ocean waves breaking on the beaches there," he told her. "Or, if you'd rather, I *think* I've got enough gas to take us all the way out to Montauk Point, where the lighthouse is, and where there'll be absolutely nothing between us and Europe but about a hundred sea gulls making a terrible racket in the sky."

"Good," she said, rubbing her hands together between her skinny legs. "That'll be neat, Dad."

At one or two o'clock that afternoon, over the remains of a seafood lunch at an outdoor, paper-plate restaurant, Evan felt calm enough to ask a few direct questions about her mother.

"Oh, she's fine," the child said, her buttery fingers still at work on a near-empty crab shell. "She's got a new job now and she really likes it a lot."

"What kind of job is that, dear?"

Asking these questions was pleasurable in itself, but Evan knew it would be a mistake to ask very many more; he would have to sense when it was time to stop.

"She's the assistant night manager at Bill Bailey's, out on Route Twelve," Kathleen told him.

"The old ice-cream parlor, you mean?"

"Yes, except it's all different now and a whole lot bigger. They've remodeled everything, and they're branching out. You can get almost anything there now, like hamburgers and french fries and stuff. Oh, and fried chicken, too, and Mom says the people there are really, really nice."

"Well, good," Evan said. "That does sound good. Listen, though, dear: you haven't told me anything about school yet. How's school?"

Small, tidy puckers of exasperation appeared in her forehead. "Dad, it's summer va*ca*tion," she said. "This is July and it's practically August and there won't even be any school again until—"

"I *know* that," he interrupted, trying for a quick save. "Don't you think I even know a thing like that? What do you take me for, some dumb, ignorant slob of a father or something? The kind of father you'd be embarrassed to introduce to your friends?"

And she was laughing now, with a sparkle in her eyes that was almost incredibly nice, but he knew better than to trust this momentary advantage. He would have to come through with something substantial and serious for her soon, or her laughter might fade into the blank, lost, bewildered look that he never knew how to interpret.

"I mean, of *course* I knew that, Kathy," he said. "All I meant, you see, is how do you feel about starting third grade? Because I know there were certain things you didn't like about second grade—a few other children you didn't much care for, and things like that—so I've been wondering how the prospect of another year of school is shaping up for you, that's all."

"Oh," Kathleen said, and she set her heaped paper plate carefully aside in the manner of someone getting down to business. "Well, I think it'll be okay most of the time—I mean, most of the other kids are perfectly nice and everything—but there's this one horrible boy."

And Evan knew at once that he was back in charge of the interview. All he had to do now was nod or frown in appropriate places while she told about the horrible boy; then he'd be expected to offer some wise-sounding advice (he could already tell how easy that part of it would be), and the two of them would be ready for the next activity of the day.

The horrible boy's name was Sonny Esposito, and he was very ugly and much too big for his age: he was so big and strong that all the other boys were afraid of him—oh, some of them might act as if they weren't, but they were—and he always laughed very loud at things that weren't even funny. Ever since way back last fall he'd done one awful thing after another to Kathleen: he had pushed her into puddles in the schoolyard; he had grabbed her best knitted hat and stuffed it far out of reach inside the ventilating system; once he had taken the classroom window pole and chased her down the hall with it until she'd had to run into the girls' room to hide from him.

"So anyway," she concluded, "on the last day of school he followed me almost all the way home, just to be mean; then he stood there in the street sort of laughing, and he said 'I haven't even started on you yet, Shepard. Just wait'll next year.'"

And for the space of at least a breath or two, Evan couldn't bring his attention into focus on anything but the boy's having called her "Shepard." Years ago, soon after the divorce, the Donovans had tactfully let him know of Mary's decision to resume the use of her maiden name, for college and for any other personal or legal requirements likely to arise; since then he had always assumed that his daughter's name must be Donovan, too, and so this came as a revelation. Son of a bitch: Kathleen Shepard.

"Well, Kathy," he began, "I don't think that's necessarily anything to worry about. Maybe all this boy's been trying to do is tell you he likes you a whole lot. Ever think of that?"

But her quick, sour expression made clear that the very idea was preposterous. "Oh, *Dad,*" she said.

"No, I'm serious," he told her. "I'm serious. Listen: when I was a boy I was always horrible to the girls I liked best. And what I think it amounted to was—"

"You were?"

"I sure was. And what I think it amounted to was this: I figured if I could make an impression on a girl—any kind of impression—then that would be better than no impression at all. So. Know what you might try doing with this Sonny Esposito?"

"What?"

"You might try being sort of nice to him. Oh, not too nice —I'm not saying that—and not even *very* nice, for that matter; just sort of courteous, in a quiet way. Like on the first day of school you might say 'Hello, Sonny,' and see what happens. I wouldn't be surprised if he starts being courteous to you, too, from then on. See how that could work out?"

Kathleen appeared to be thinking it over. "Well—maybe," she said at last, though she didn't sound at all persuaded, and there was a forgiving tolerance in her hesitant smile. She seemed to be saying she should have known how useless his advice would be in a matter like this, but that she didn't really mind because he was a father well worth having in other ways.

It took him a moment to remember where else he had seen a smile like that: it was Mary's own way of looking at him, in the best of their early times, whenever he'd solemnly spoken his mind on some complicated question without coming close to the heart of it—and that touch of forgiveness in her eyes had always been a lovely, shining thing.

Now, though, he was afraid he'd taken too soft a line on Sonny Esposito. His own most vivid memories of being horrible to girls were of a much later time in childhood, of the sixth and seventh and eighth grades and beyond; he couldn't honestly say what his behavior had been like at Kathleen's age, and shouldn't have pretended he could. Besides, what if Sonny Esposito really was some menacing, overgrown Italian whelp that any other girl's father would instantly detest?

"I think that's worth a try anyway, dear," he said, "don't you? Being sort of nice to him? But if he still goes on giving you trouble I want you to tell me about it right away. Okay? You promise?"

"Well, okay," she said uncertainly.

"Because then I'll call the principal and arrange for this boy to be given a very sharp reprimand. Or," he said, warming to his own voice, "I might just pay a visit to that classroom of yours myself, and I'd find him there and take him out in the hall, and I'd say 'Look, Esposito: You better leave my little girl alone or you're gonna be in trouble, understand? Bad trouble.' "

"Oh, *Dad.*"

"Whaddya mean?"

"I don't know, it's just silly, is all. Nobody's father ever does things like that."

"So what does anybody's father ever do?"

"I don't know."

"Well, but I mean what was the point of telling me about this boy, Kathy, if you didn't want a few suggestions?"

"I don't know." She was gazing off into the distance of the highway now, watching the cars, and he could see just enough of her face to tell it had taken on its lost, bewildered look.

"Talk about silly," he said. "Seems to me you can be pretty silly yourself sometimes." And then, clearly, it was time to change the subject. "Feel like getting back on the road again?" he asked her. "And maybe find some things to do along the way?"

" 'Kay."

He didn't quite know what he meant by "things to do along the way" except a roadside game of miniature golf that they'd both grown bored with in previous outings; still, as a last resort they could always visit a big, cut-rate toy store not far from her home.

When she said goodbye to him at last and turned away to the dim face of her grandparents' house, conspicuously using both arms to carry the few cheap things he'd bought for her, Evan watched for the slow arm wave behind the screen and answered it with a jauntier, more youthful wave of his own; then he walked back to the car.

There was always a great sadness on these homeward drives; sometimes too there were feelings of inadequacy ("So what does anybody's father ever do?") and of failure. Oh, Jesus, divorce could sure as hell leave a lot to be desired.

For a while he just drove north toward Cold Spring Harbor, putting on a little speed because he'd be late for dinner if he didn't, but soon an unaccustomed thought occurred to him: the hell with dinner. The Drakes could eat without him for once; they might even be happier, in fact, if he didn't show up.

He skillfully found his way to Route Twelve, made the turn, and began driving east in what anyone would have said was no particular hurry. But he wouldn't have tried to kid anyone about where he was headed now, and he sure as God wasn't trying to kid himself. When the long bright structure of Bill Bailey's emerged from a clutter of other commercial ventures, under a darkening sky, he saw at once that Kathleen had been right: it was a far more impressive business than the simple place he'd remembered. Mary must have pretty nice working conditions here, if being "assistant night manager" kept her well enough away from the heat and bustle of service personnel out in front where the quick snacks and the money changed hands.

He was slowing down to make the turn with other hungry customers when it struck him that he'd better not do this: it wouldn't be a good idea. She worked only at night and it wasn't even night yet; somebody would tell him either to come back later or to wait—and if he decided to wait, in some spotless, airless alcove, he'd be as tense and jumpy as a nervous wreck by the time she came walking in and discovered him there. No, the better plan would be to find some other place along the road for waiting—or, if he continued to feel the almost crippling doubts at work in him now, to turn around right here and go home. He could always come again some other night, after dark, when he had a better grip on his courage.

So he went all the way home, where Rachel had kept his dinner warm. And he allowed three or four more days and nights to pass—patience was important in a thing like this —before he felt brave enough to make another try.

"Are you going out, darling?" Rachel asked when she came upstairs that night and found him fresh from the shower, putting on a clean shirt; and her large-eyed, small-mouthed face showed she wasn't even trying to hide her uneasiness.

"Well, just to get away from the house for a while," he said. "Just to be by myself for a little while, is all. Nothing wrong with that, is there?"

She assured him there was nothing wrong with it at all, which seemed to lend a certain sanction to his escapade, and twenty minutes later, as he hummed along toward the lights of Route Twelve, he vowed that this time there would be no turning back.

Each of the hurrying boys and girls who worked at the take-out section of Bill Bailey's wore an overseas cap of starched white gauze, so flimsy a thing that the girls had to attach it to their hair with bobby pins, and they all looked much too busy to be approached with any questions other than those in the line of business. But then Evan saw a middle-aged woman hovering behind them in a way that suggested she was their supervisor, so he edged in, leaned a little over the counter, and called to her in a polite shout.

"Excuse me, ma'am, do you know where I can find Miss Donovan? Mary Donovan?"

"No, I don't know of anyone by that name. Sorry."

"Or maybe," he said, "maybe she's called Mary Shepard here."

"Oh, Mary *Shep*ard," the woman said. "Well, certainly. Mary's up on the second floor. Will you step around to the side door then? So I can let you in?"

It felt funny to be welcomed into the management side of a customer-service counter, like being allowed behind the tellers' windows of a bank, and funny to be shown up a lighted plank staircase that smelled of fresh lumber and looked as raw and finger-smudged as it must have been the day the carpenters hammered it together. Then he was at the partly open door of a little office with unpainted beaverboard walls, and he could see Mary alone in there, standing at a file cabinet. She was facing away from him, but he recognized her at once by the bright, loose hair and the legs; all he had to do was give the door a shove to open it all the way.

"Well, *Ev*an," she said. "Well, I—What're you—Well, what a surprise."

It was a surprise, all right. He was surprised at how steady and self-confident he felt when she sat down at a desk and offered him the chair beside it; he was surprised too at the ease and friendliness in the first few exchanges of their talk. As if to prove how much they still had in common, they had fallen at once into discussing Kathleen and agreeing on what a nice, smart little girl she was turning out to be.

"And she really does enjoy the time she spends with you, Evan," Mary told him. "She talks about you quite a lot."

"Well, good," he said. "That's really—that's very good to hear."

When he asked her out for a drink she examined her wristwatch—he'd forgotten what shapely forearms she had —and said "Well, I won't be through here for another hour, but sure. I mean I really would like to have a drink then, if you don't mind waiting."

And he didn't mind at all. Downstairs and outdoors and alone again, back in the trampled dust in front of the place, he pitied the drab supervisor and all her quick, harried, frowning children because none of them looked as though they had anything worth waiting for, tonight or ever.

Smoking more cigarettes than he wanted, he killed most of the hour in his parked car with the engine running, trying to get a halfway decent sound or even a resonant buzz out of the dashboard radio. It had never worked for him, this cramped, crappy little radio set; it probably hadn't worked for most of this car's previous owners either, though it must once have been the pride of whoever first drove the damned car away from a dealer's showroom, only a couple of years ago.

By the end of the hour he was nervously alert, watching the door at this end of Bill Bailey's, and when Mary finally did appear there he cut the engine and sprang from the car to greet her.

"My God," she said. "Is this really your car? Is it new?"

"Oh, it's a 'forty," he said bashfully, "but it was practically a wreck when I picked it up; had to do an awful lot of work on it, front end and back. Got it running pretty good now, though."

"Well, I'm not surprised," she said, and there was a subtle suggestion of teasing in her eyes. "You've always been something of a genius with cars, haven't you."

She told him there was a fairly nice place called Oliver's a mile or two up the road; the only problem was that she'd have to take her car there, too, so she could drive it home later and have it for work tomorrow. Could he sort of follow her, then, in this lovely great machine of his?

"Be glad to, ma'am." He whipped the fingers of his right hand up as if to touch the visor of an imaginary chauffeur's cap and was briefly reminded of his shitty little brother-in-law, though Mary seemed to find it a charming gesture: she narrowed her eyes to give him a small, bright laugh and assured him it wouldn't take long.

"Well, but we were only kids then, Evan," she explained half an hour later, over her second drink in one of the deep semicircular booths at Oliver's. "We might as well've been twelve or thirteen years old when we—you know—when we got married. Doesn't it seem that way to you?"

He was looking around this voluptuous little place, or trying to, and wondering why they kept the lighting down to near-total darkness. (Were you expected to snuggle up and smooch in here? Was it the kind of place where you could finger-fuck your girl while the jukebox throbbed and moaned into some sappy little song about love in wartime?)

"Well, okay, sure," he said. "But then, why'd you take my name back, and give it to Kathy too?"

"Oh, I wouldn't attach much significance to that if I were you," she said in the same explanatory, advisory tone. "It was just something I did a few years ago when she started school. Seemed silly not to at the time, and besides I think I always have liked 'Shepard' better, as far as names go."

He wasn't doing very well—that much was clear—but at least their talk hadn't yet begun to weaken and falter; it was still alive. Anyone happening to glance over into their part of the darkness would have said they were having a good-enough time together.

"So whatever happened to the dentist?" he asked her.

"What dentist is that?"

"You know. Your mother told me once you were engaged to a dental student."

"Oh, my God. That was years and *years* ago, back in I think my freshman year; and we certainly weren't 'engaged' —that could only have been something my mother misunderstood. She hardly ever gets things straight, as you may know."

This struck him as a good-enough chance for saying Well, so how many other guys have there been? Or, So who do you have for a man now? But he hadn't managed to frame either question in his mind before she spoke first.

"No, but how about you, Evan? What's your wife like?"

"Well, she's—sweet," he told her. "She's very sweet, and I guess that's part of the trouble. She's like a little girl—*is* a little girl. And I mean we were okay when we had our own place down in Amityville; we were fine then, but now we're living with her crazy old mother and her shitty little— Look, Mary, I'd really rather not go into all this right now, is that okay?"

"Well, of course it is," she said. "Anything you want to tell or not tell is perfectly okay with me."

But Evan hadn't meant to reveal anywhere near that much about his personal life to this girl, and now he felt stupid for shooting his mouth off.

One advantage of the very low lighting in this room, he'd decided, was that it could make almost any girl look like a million dollars. If he could only be quiet now and try to relax in the subtle company of the way this particular girl was made to look—the lovely, half-mocking eyes, the fine cheekbones and the rich cascading hair—it might still be possible to settle for a good-enough time. And what the hell other kind of time could he ever have been dumb enough to expect? "Care for another drink?" he asked her.

"Well, no, it's getting late," she said, in what he had to admit was a nice-enough way. But then, as if for no other purpose than to let his heart and lungs begin working again, she said "I was wondering, though, if you might like to see my apartment—it's just sort of around the corner— and we could have a nightcap there."

As he followed her car down a long straight macadam

road between potato fields (and for the second time tonight he was glad her car was nothing but a dusty little heap out of the early thirties because it seemed to suggest she hadn't yet been taken up by some rich bastard), Evan Shepard knew he would have to consider himself the horse's ass and clown of the century if he let this girl get away.

Her apartment turned out to be the downstairs half of what had once been a potato farmer's home, and she'd given it a dauntingly intellectual look with shelved books and phonograph albums on almost every wall. But Evan suspected these college-girl trappings wouldn't matter at all if he could make his move soon—maybe even now, while she reached up to open her liquor cabinet—and he was right. All he had to do was get close enough to touch her waist, saying "Mary," and she turned around and belonged to him again.

"Oh, this is funny," she said in his arms. For just a second he thought she meant to twist and pull free, but instead she said "Oh, this is really funny, isn't it. Oh, Evan . . ."

They tripped or stumbled and sank onto a college-graduate's setup of mattress and box springs—a "studio couch" —and when they struggled up from it, as if fighting for air, it was only to rid themselves of summer clothes.

And oh, it might be funny as hell but it was happening; it was true: he was in love with Mary all over again. Oh, here were the tits that had driven him wild in high school, and the marvelous legs, and here was the sweet dampening bush and the mound of her, alive in his hand. Oh, Jesus; oh, Mary . . .

"Evan," she kept saying. "Oh, Evan Shepard . . ."

They took their time, making it last as long as they knew how, finding no need to be apart until long after it was over.

Lying on his back and blinking as his breath came back to normal, Evan began to wish they hadn't left the lights on in this roomful of learning and culture, and he hoped Mary

would be the first to start talking again. But she only padded quickly into the bathroom and stayed there long
enough to let him sort out his clothes in a befuddled way.
When she came out, wearing a knee-length cotton robe, he
was up and dressed and squinting at the titles of books
along one wall.

"Coffee?" she asked.

And at least they could have coffee in her kitchen, where
there weren't any emblems of anybody's higher-than-aver-
age intelligence. After a minute or two he was almost at
ease with her again, and he could already sense how he'd
feel on the road going home: he would feel like the very
devil of a man.

". . . Well, I heard about your draft status, Evan," Mary
was saying across her kitchen table, "and of course I was
glad for Kathy, but I was sorry, too, because I thought
you'd probably want to be in the service."

"Yeah, well, you're right, but what the hell; there's nothing anybody can do about it. Besides, that's ancient history
now. I don't even think about it much any more, from—you
know—from day to day."

"Good," she said. "It's always important to keep the day-
to-day stuff separate from the ancient history, isn't it."

When he was ready to leave she got up and gave him a
discreet, oddly restrained embrace at the kitchen door.

"Oh, Jesus, Mary, this was nice," he said against her hair.
"Be okay if I come over again sometime? I mean if I call you
first?"

Her answer was a little too long in the making. "Well, I
guess so, sure," she said at last, "as long as you don't make
a habit of it."

And that was the only sour note, the only sharply disappointing part of the night that rode in his memory all the
way home and all the next day at the plant.

"Don't make a habit of it" was something only a chilly

girl, only a "tough" girl would think of saying, and Evan knew it would stay with him for days because never in any of their old times together—not even in the worst of their fights—had he really thought of Mary as being that kind of girl.

11

Rachel came carefully downstairs one morning, in a dressing gown that wasn't quite clean, and stood at the brink of the living room as though preparing to make an announcement. She looked around at each member of the double household—at Evan, who was soberly opening the morning paper, at Phil, who'd been home from Costello's for hours but hadn't felt like sleeping yet, and at her mother, who was setting the table for breakfast—and then she came out with it.

"I love everybody," she said, stepping into the room with an uncertain smile. And her declaration might have had the generally soothing effect she'd intended if her mother hadn't picked it up and exploited it for all the sentimental weight it would bear.

"Oh, Rachel," she cried, "what a sweet, lovely thing to say!" and she turned to address Evan and Phil as if both of them might be too crass or numbskulled to appreciate it by themselves. "Isn't that a wonderful thing for this girl to say, on a perfectly ordinary Friday morning? Rachel, I think you've put us all to shame for our petty bickering and our selfish little silences, and it's something I'll never forget. You really do have a marvelous wife, Evan, and I have a marvelous daughter. Oh, and Rachel, you can be sure that everybody in this house loves you, too, and we're all tremendously glad to have you feeling so well."

Rachel's embarrassment was now so intense that it seemed almost to prevent her from taking her place at the table; she tried two quick, apologetic looks at her husband and her brother, but they both missed the message in her eyes.

And Gloria wasn't yet quite finished. "I honestly believe that was a moment we'll remember all our lives," she said. "Little Rachel coming downstairs—or little *big* Rachel, rather—and saying 'I love everybody.' You know what I wish, though, Evan? I only wish your father could've been here this morning to share it with us."

But by then even Gloria seemed to sense that the thing had been carried far enough. As soon as she'd stopped talking the four of them took their breakfast in a hunched and businesslike silence, until Phil mumbled "Excuse me" and shoved back his chair.

"Where do you think you're going, young man?" Gloria inquired. "I don't think you'd better go anywhere until you finish up all of that egg."

"Well, but frankly, dear," Charles Shepard was saying at his own breakfast table, across the village, "I've about run out of excuses. And it might be so much easier than you think. We'd put in an appearance over there, is all—just once—and then it would be done with."

But Grace only said she still saw no reason why they couldn't bring the woman over here instead. "Wouldn't that take care of it? And wouldn't it be more reasonable anyway, as long as she knows I'm housebound?"

"No, it wouldn't," Charles told her. He had tried to explain before that he didn't want to invite Gloria Drake here because they'd have no control over how long she might stay—and, worse, because she might then feel free to come dropping in on other afternoons, again and again. Now he began explaining it once more, patiently, but Grace was in too peevish a mood to listen.

"Oh, that's silly," she said. "That's nonsense. And I really don't think you'd be hectoring me this way, Charles, if you knew what it does to my blood pressure."

So he stopped hectoring her. When she was ready to retire to the sun porch for the day he helped her walk there very slowly, with one arm around her back for safety, as if she might fall.

Except for Evan and a few very close neighbors, Charles had always felt alone in knowing that Grace wasn't really "housebound" at all. Several times a year, if there was a movie she especially wanted to see, she would insist on his taking her to see it and would even hurry him up the dim movie-house stairway to the balcony, where smoking was permitted, and he would glance furtively around the audience up there in fear of being seen by people he knew from the village—people from the grocery store, say, or from the laundry.

He felt sure he could eventually persuade her to agree with him in the matter of visiting Gloria Drake, but this wasn't the day for it. All he could do this morning, after getting her settled on the chaise longue with her light summer blanket and her magazine, was go into the kitchen and fix her morning drink.

Phil Drake got very little sleep that day. He kept wrestling and punching his pillow into different shapes, as if that would help, but whenever a wave of sleep overcame him it brought ugly dreams of the kind that children have in fever, and they'd quickly wake him again. Then he'd be at the mercy of random, disorderly waking thoughts that made no sense. Nothing made sense, and he was reminded of times at school when he'd sit for an hour and a half in the near-perfect silence of study hall without turning a page of his textbook or even reading a line of it.

On his first day in this house his mother had used her forefinger to part the dotted-swiss curtain on Evan and Rachel's bedroom door ("Oh, good; she's awake") and ever since then, without wanting to think about it, he had known how easy it would be to have a look at them getting laid. The opportunity was there every night and almost every afternoon—and since he'd been working at Costello's it was there in the early mornings too—but it had always seemed less a temptation than a mockery or parody of what all such temptations implied. He knew he would never be the kind of creep who did things like that, and so there had often been a slight, automatic lift of his self-esteem when he walked past the lightly curtained door.

Then this morning, home from work and poking around the house because he didn't yet feel like going to bed, watching the daylight break into every other room but theirs, he had found himself thinking seriously about that door and its curtain. He had even gone to stand there for a while, scarcely breathing, with one finger extended an inch or two from the fabric, just to find out how it would feel to come that close to doing an unforgivable thing; and in turning away he knew he could no longer consider this a mockery or parody: it was temptation itself.

Now, though, lying sleepless and waiting for the day to pass, he felt incapable of putting together any coherent thoughts at all except the bleak and persistent idea that nothing in the world made sense. There was no sense to be made of forces and events in this house, and nothing would make sense at the parking lot tonight either, when he padded around collecting his quarters and dimes. It probably wasn't much more than a beggar's job anyway: if he stopped showing up there every night he doubted if anyone would notice. Drivers would park their cars in the right places; the "planning" would take care of itself; people would find their way in and out of the restaurant without the help of Phil Drake's goofy flashlight. Still, going to work would be better than staying home.

Rachel was alone in the kitchen—it was her turn to cook —so it was she who gave him his supper there, and that was a good thing because he felt he couldn't have put up with his mother's company tonight.

"Well, I'm pretty sure I'll be having the baby before you go back to school," she said, "so at least you'll—you know —get to know each other a little."

"Yeah; well, I hope so."

Maybe it was true that Rachel loved everybody; if not, or not quite, she certainly knew how to give a convincing performance.

"And you mustn't mind if Evan seems a little abrupt and rude these days. I think it's mostly that he doesn't quite care for the idea of becoming a father—of becoming a father *again*, that is—but he'll get used to it."

And Phil assured her that he understood.

His time at Costello's that night was little more than a

daydreaming or sleepwalking through the job, and not long after midnight he made his first dumb mistake of the summer.

The left-hand border of the parking lot was indistinct—you couldn't say where the restaurant's property ended and the shadowed part of the lot belonging to a Gulf station began—and the manager had cautioned Phil about that tricky place the day he took the job. It might work to Phil's advantage on busy nights, he explained, when you could fit three or four extra cars along the far side of the invisible line—the guys at the Gulf station would probably never complain—but Phil ought to be on the lookout for high-school couples who might want to park there just to "park." If possible he should use the flashlight to discourage them even from pulling into that area—they all ought to know by now that it wasn't any lovers' lane—but once they were settled out there it was probably best to leave them the hell alone.

The trouble tonight was that he wandered too far into the tricky place and opened the passenger's door of a car filled with sex: one couple writhing in the front seat and another in back. An open bottle of whiskey fell out at his feet and dribbled into the pebbles; there was a glimpse of a girl's bare tits before she shrieked and covered herself, and the other girl in back called "Well, hel*lo,* Galahad," in a voice that sounded too deep and husky for high school—all this before he shut the door again and started to walk away as if nothing had happened. For ten or twelve paces he expected one or both of the boys, or men, to rush him from behind and spin him around and beat the shit out of him, and when he made a clean getaway he guessed it was only because there'd been enough light to let them see how young and foolishly innocent he was. The car soon started up, made its turn on Gulf station property and sped away into the distance of Route Nine, but Phil was still trembling for a long time afterwards, and the flashlight was clammy with sweat in his hand. He felt stupid—the only saving grace was that nobody from Costello's had caught him in his blunder—and for the rest of the night he forced himself to stay alert whether his memory was haunted by the girl's tits or not.

At three thirty, half an hour before quitting time, the service-entrance door swung open to cast a yellow light across the lot, and a hoarse old voice called out to him. "Hey, kid, wanna come on in?" It was the gaunt dishwasher who'd once called him a sad case, but this was plainly another kind of occasion.

"Well, but I'm supposed to stay out here until—"

"Ah, fuck the cars. This is more important."

Everything inside the service door was brightly and buoyantly alive: they were having a party for Aaron because this was his last night's work before going into the army.

The kitchen and pantry were packed with well-wishers—even the night manager was there with a drink in his hand, laughing—and Aaron moved happily among them, shaking hands, pausing to kiss the girls in a decorous way. He still wore the white shirt and black bow tie of his job, but his apron had been flung into the laundry hamper for the last time.

"Well, hey there, Phil, glad to see you," he said in passing, and Phil was pleased that he'd remembered his name.

Wooden duckboards from the kitchen floor were stacked against one wall to make a little stage; the Portuguese headwaiter climbed onto it and reached down to help Aaron up to stand beside him; then all the party sounds were hushed as the headwaiter gave an introductory speech, so heavily accented that only a few phrases of it were clear: ". . . our high esteem . . . our continuing admiration . . . our profound best wishes." Next came a presentation, by one of the waitresses, of two gifts for which all employees except Phil had evidently chipped in: a silver wristwatch and a silver serviceman's identification bracelet. And when the applause had faded again it was time for Aaron, still flushed with thanks and embarrassment, to say a few words.

"Well, I don't quite know what to say," he began, "except to thank you all—and I mean really thank you, with all my heart. Oh, and I'm glad my girlfriend Judy is here with us tonight, too, because I'm always trying to think up new ways of impressing her, and this is the best one yet. Up to now it's mostly been a matter of dropping hints about what a hotshot football player I was, and the trouble with that one is it's never been true: I was a very mediocre player. Even in my senior year I only got into two or three games when our side was ahead by about thirty-six points, but I always figured she'd never find out because we went to different high schools fourteen miles apart and we didn't even know each other then. So anyway, there are the facts, honey"—here he turned briefly to a laughing girl at the front of the crowd—"and I can't tell you what a relief it is that I'll never have to fall back on that line of bragging again.

"No, but the main thing I feel tonight, apart from great friendship for all of you—oh, and apart from knowing how much I'm going to miss you all, the whole time I'm away—the main thing is I couldn't have dreamed of a nicer good-bye.

"I don't suppose any man knows what to expect in the army. There've been plenty of movies about it, but the movies don't even pretend to show the truth about the army and the war, any more than they ever show the truth about love.

"I hope I'll be assigned to the infantry because I've always liked the idea of it; then if they ever do make an invasion of Europe I hope I'll be sent there, instead of the Pacific, because all my people are Jewish. Still, you never know; I might wind up as a supply clerk or a payroll clerk in Nebraska or someplace like that.

"Well, I know I'm talking too much, but I'm almost finished. The only other thing I want to say is—I want to say God bless you. God bless you all, dear friends, and goodnight."

A few of the girls were crying as they helped to swell the long, cheering ovation, and young Judy climbed up on the platform to embrace him and to press her face against his sweated shirt.

With the party ringing all the way home in his head, Phil Drake was almost ready to believe once again that things could make sense in the world; and if nothing else he knew he was going to sleep like a fool.

Rachel was alone in the living room that evening, seated comfortably under a good lamp with a sewing basket that might have been chosen as a prop to make her seem the very picture of a contented young wife, when Phil came downstairs.

"Evan go out?" he asked her. "Where'd he go?"

"I don't know," she said, and then after snipping a piece of thread with her teeth she gave him a more complete reply. "I don't know where he's going because I didn't ask. Not even married couples have to know everything about each other all the time, you see. We all deserve a little privacy now and then, don't you think?"

"Oh, well, sure," Phil said quickly. "I didn't mean to sound as if I—well, sure, I know. Of course."

Then their mother came in from the kitchen, absently touching up her hair, and said "Has Evan gone out, dear? Where's he going?"

Even with occasional traffic lights turning against him, Evan made excellent time across the great flat width of the Island. He was almost to the intersection of Route Twelve before he stopped to make the necessary call at an outdoor telephone booth.

"Would it be 'making a habit of it,' " he inquired, "if I come over to your place tonight?"

"Well, I wouldn't say I've had more than my *share* of men," Mary was saying as they lolled conversationally in her bed a few hours later, "but I wouldn't want to say I've had less than my share either."

She was lying on her back with the top sheet drawn up an inch above her nipples, not even seeming aware of what a tantalizing sight that made, and Evan was a little sorry he'd gotten her started on this particular line of talk.

"And I think I've done about my share of the dumping, too," she said, "rather than being dumped. No, but the only one I might've married was this young lawyer I worked for, in the first job I had after college. We were together about a year and I thought it was really wonderful until he came home from a trip to Kansas City and told me he was in love with an airline stewardess. The funny part was I didn't believe him—I thought he was kidding—but he wasn't, so there wasn't anything to do but get out of that office and take the first job I could find, with some dumb little chain of drugstores in Hempstead; that only lasted a few months before I went to work at Bailey's, so now you know practically everything."

In exchange for that information she wanted, pleasantly, to hear more about the time of his engagement to Rachel, and soon he had blundered into letting her know the most regrettable part of the story.

"Oh," she said when his voice had faltered and stopped. "So you didn't get laid until after the wedding."

"Well, I mean we sort of did. Yes and no. Look, it's hard to explain, okay?" And now he was stuck with having to explain it. "Our first time was when I took her to some lousy old hotel on West Twenty-fifth Street, and I think the hotel was a bad mistake in itself. She was so shy and frightened and terrifically nervous up in that room that I got very nervous too, in some funny way that I couldn't even figure out, and we didn't really—you know—we didn't do very well together. Then the other times were when I borrowed an apartment in Jackson Heights from this guy I know at the plant, only neither of those times were a hell of a lot better. So by then I was ready to think Well, okay, what the hell? Why *not* get married right away, then, and let the sex part of it take care of itself in time. Do you see?"

"Sure."

"So that's what we did. I think everything took care of itself within a couple of nights, and we've been perfectly fine ever since. And I mean we're perfectly fine now, except I keep wishing we could've made a stronger start. I think she does too."

And if Mary were really a tough girl she might have laughed then, but there wasn't any laughter in her thoughtful face.

"Well, I think it's sad when anyone feels this pressure to get married," she said. "Even if I were pregnant again I don't think I'd feel any extra-special need to get married. I *like* being single, you see. I like the freedom of it and the way it keeps teaching me new things about myself. I suppose that's an attitude I learned in college."

"Yeah, well, and so what the hell else did you learn in college? How to read all these fucking books? How to make your bed six inches off the fucking floor?"

He rolled heavily away from her, got up with some difficulty, and made for the kitchen to get more beer. He was furious without quite knowing why: maybe because he'd told her all that embarrassing stuff—it was never a good idea to spill your guts to a girl—or maybe because she'd spent a year in love with a lawyer.

"Well, Evan," she said quietly, "I think college might help broaden your own perspectives quite a lot; or would you rather be a mechanic all your life?"

He turned on her in the kitchen doorway. "I'm not a mechanic," he told her with a fierce pride of trade. "I'm a machinist."

But after making that one important distinction (and she *should* have known better than to say "mechanic," for Christ's sake) he found he wasn't angry any more. Bringing two cold beers back into the main room, he said he was sorry; then he told her he fully intended to go to college as soon as he could afford it. "And I may have enough by next year this time, because we've been saving money on a regular basis right along—every week; every month."

Her bed looked too low to sit on, so he took his beer to one of the only two chairs in the room and tried to settle there instead; but he wished he had a bathrobe because it felt funny to be sitting bare-assed in a chair.

"Oh, I hope it does work out for you, Evan," she was saying. "And I know you'll love the life of it, once you get started. It sort of opens up whole new worlds for you, in ways you couldn't possibly have imagined before."

"Yeah, well, I've heard that part. Every college graduate I've ever met wants to tell me about the new worlds opening up. You people all have the same line, whether you know it or not. It's like talking to a member of the Communist Party."

And that seemed to strike her as funny enough to elicit a sweet, bright ripple of laughter. He had almost forgotten how nice it could be to see Mary laugh like that, with her eyes dancing. Then he was back in bed with her, where he belonged: he had flipped the top sheet down to her knees and he was having her again, as if she were the only girl he had ever known.

Sometime later, when he was getting dressed to go home, she said "Oh, it's such a pleasure just to watch you walk and turn and move around; it always has been. And you know what else I used to love? I loved to watch you get into your car and drive away—just because it meant you knew exactly what you were doing, and because you always did it so well."

12

"Charles?" Grace Shepard said at lunch one day. "I suppose I might as well go and meet Mrs. Drake this afternoon, if you're still determined to take me there."

And her statement sounded so deceptively casual that he didn't trust it at first. He tried to look as though he were thinking it over; then he said "Well, as long as you're willing, dear, I can just as easily arrange it for tomorrow, or for sometime over the weekend; wouldn't that be better?"

"No, let's do it today," she said, "and get it over with."

She had ignored her breakfast and only picked at her lunch, while smoking heavily all morning; that was one way he could tell she'd had to fortify herself before making her decision, and now the early hours of the afternoon would require her to fortify herself still further.

But it was almost the first of August now; he had long grown tired of his own argument, and he knew he'd better take advantage of her rare social bravery while it lasted.

He helped her get settled on the sun porch again—"Now, then; why don't you just think about the nice clothes you're going to wear this afternoon, and I'll come and get you in plenty of time to go upstairs and change"—then, after the table was cleared and the dishes scraped and stacked for washing, he called Gloria Drake and told her they'd be over sometime after four.

He found other things to do in the kitchen when the dishes were done—you could always find work in a kitchen if you wanted it to work for you. Once he nipped into the dining room and checked the liquor supply in the sideboard, just to see if he'd made the right assumption about all that fortifying, and he had. A quart of bourbon, placed here last night with its seal still unbroken, was now less than half full. Well, it might be a tricky afternoon, but there was no getting out of it now.

In another section of Cold Spring Harbor, a world away, Harriet Talmage was seriously vexed with her grandson for what seemed the first time in years. He was pacing back and forth in front of her chair and making wide, theatrical gestures with his arms as if she were impossible to reason with, while it seemed increasingly clear to her that he was the one beyond reason.

"Well, because I don't especially *like* the woman, Gerard, that's why," she said. "I found her rather tiresome that day, as I must surely have told you at the time, and I saw no point in having any further—any further connection with her."

"But isn't that kind of rude, though? Just dumping a person that way?"

"I don't see any element of rudeness at all," she told him. "I was perfectly pleasant when she asked us over there last month, or whenever it was; I simply said I'd made other plans for the afternoon but that I hoped we'd keep in touch."

"So? Won't this just be keeping in touch? Dropping in for an hour or two? Where's the harm in that?"

"Well, it's hardly a question of 'harm,' Gerard. And I can't imagine why you're persisting in this argument. If it's so terribly important to see the Drake boy, why can't you simply ride over there on your bicycle?"

"Because it'll be *nicer* this way, is all, don't you see? Like the time they came here? Going there alone would be too obvious."

And his saying "too obvious" gave it all away. He was still at an age when an unpopular boy might need to pursue other boys as craftily as if they were girls, and his long unhappiness at school must have taught him, harshly, that being too obvious was the worst mistake you could make. It was almost enough to break her heart.

Very seldom, in raising her daughter's only child, had Harriet felt any real confidence that she was doing it well— there had been so many unexpected difficulties and so many hasty settlings for the easiest way. Now that he'd become a courteous deep-voiced adolescent she often felt she could take some pride in her earlier judgments after all, but at moments like this she knew better.

And in a few more years, when he'd begin to fall in love with girls, he would probably bring far too much emotional intensity to every new attachment. He'd be the kind of boy who could frighten a girl with unwarranted possessiveness, the kind of boy who would say things like "How do you *know* you don't love me?" And if no girl could bear him very long he might slip down among less and less desirable girls until he'd settle for some dim little girl of the wrong kind and possibly the wrong class as well; then he might easily spend his life as one of those slack, amiable, underdeveloped men that everyone feels sorry for.

Well, but even so, the drifting pattern of the way he was could scarcely be resolved in this one insecure afternoon: his next important lesson in manliness would have to wait.

"Oh, well, dear," she said at last, "if it really means that much to you, of course we'll go together. Why don't you tell Ralph to have the car ready at four thirty, then."

Charles's phone call hadn't given Gloria enough time to do very much about straightening up the living room, so she'd chosen to attend to her clothes and her hair instead. Then from a window, peering through hanging foliage that gave her only a partial view of the driveway, she saw the Shepards' cab arrive. She saw Charles get out and turn back to help a slow, surprisingly bulky woman settle one foot and then the other on the ground. When they began walking toward the house together, bending under low branches, Gloria couldn't suppress a tremor of satisfaction at how fat Grace was, but at closer range the afternoon light came to play on Grace's face and it was lovely. Anyone could see now where Evan's good looks had come from.

"Well, at last," Gloria said. "How awfully nice to meet you at last, Grace." She wondered if she ought to reach out and give her a kiss—wouldn't that be appropriate, under the circumstances?—but an almost imperceptible flinching in Grace's smile held her back, so she moved to the liquor table and busied herself there, talking steadily.

". . . And I'm afraid everything's sort of disorderly here today; we've been trying to rearrange the furniture in different ways but we haven't decided on anything definite yet, as you can see. . . ."

But at least Phil was here, being polite in his best private-school manner, making a good impression, and Rachel would be coming downstairs at any minute. It was always gratifying for Gloria, in times of social tension, to know that her children were presentable; she was reminded now of that first day in New York when she might have talked herself weak and sick in her fascination with the Shepard men, trying and trying to hold their interest, if the children hadn't come home just in time to save her.

". . . Oh, Costello's, of course," Grace was saying. "And the old Island Palace, a little farther out. Do you know the Palace?"

"No, I'm afraid I—"

Then Rachel came in, seeming to parade her pregnancy in a fresh maternity dress, and said "Oh, Grace!" with an enthusiasm that struck Gloria as excessive until she realized Rachel had probably come to be on affectionate terms with her during the leisurely weekends of her engagement.

"You look wonderful, dear," Grace said. "You look like the very picture of a healthy, happy, child-carrying girl."

"Well, thank you—and I *hope* I'm healthy; I know I've never been happier."

It seemed to Gloria that she'd never heard quite such a silly claim to personal well-being except in Academy Award ceremonies on the radio, and it made her sullen with envy and malice. It reminded her of Curtis Drake at his most vapid; but then, Rachel had always been her father's child.

"Oh, that's so good," Grace was saying, and she turned to Charles for confirmation. "Isn't it good when a wife can say a thing like that?"

He agreed that it was, and he even said it was enough to make any husband proud, but he was watching her closely now with special attention to the brilliance of her eyes. This was the high-hearted, keyed-up, "delightful" phase of her drunkenness: it would begin to dwindle soon, but there'd still be time to get her out of here and home before she sank.

"Do you know, Rachel," Grace went on, "from the moment Evan brought you out to the house that first time I knew you were the right girl for him. You'll always be the right girl."

And Rachel might have let that compliment stand, but this was evidently a day for extravagant feelings. "Well," she said, "I certainly hope you know how much I've come to love you both."

It seemed to Gloria now that these three strangers were trying to cut her off and shut her out; they wanted to make her feel alone in the world, and they might as well have been trying to kill her. But she could still fight for her life in the only way she knew: she started talking again.

"Grace?" she said, but the babble of their self-congratulating voices was so solid a barrier that she had to say it twice before she could break in. "Grace? Has Charles ever told you how we all met, back in the city? And the funny, wonderful way we—"

"Oh, the car breaking down," Grace Shepard said. "Yes, that's a marvelous story. It's funny, though, you know; people talk about 'chance meetings' but there's really no such thing because *every* meeting is a matter of chance, isn't that true? Especially between a boy and a girl? Even the most carefully planned, carefully arranged meeting you can imagine—the way Charles and I met, for example. I was great friends then with another girl who told me I would absolutely have to come out to a dance at Fort Devens because there was a boy there she knew I was going to love. So I went—not even *wanting* to go, especially, because I was practically engaged to another boy at the time—and there he was, this perfect dream of a young lieutenant, and I loved him at once and I've never been sorry in all these years."

"Yes, well, that's—lovely," Gloria said. "That's really wonderful." But all she knew for certain, looking into this glowing, aging face, was that she wished Grace Shepard were dead.

"What's this?" Rachel cried. "There's this big—this big limousine kind of car in the driveway."

Phil went quickly to the window and then turned on his mother. "Did you invite *them* today?"

"No, I didn't," she said in all innocence, as though he ought to know she wouldn't do a thing like that without consulting him, but then she said "Still, I think it's *nice* to have the kind of house where people feel free to drop in any time, don't you?" And she felt a little frightened but essentially glad. Nobody in this family group would make mistakes of the kind that Harriet Talmage might take to heart; and if Harriet Talmage was surprised at first to find herself in this shabby room, with its insulation-board walls, it wouldn't be long before she discovered what superior people they all were.

"Well, Harriet *Tal*mage," she said in the doorway. "How very nice to see you. And Flash. Do come and join us. I can't offer you tea, I'm afraid, because we've all been having a drink. This is my daughter Rachel; this is her mother-in-law, Mrs. Shepard, and Captain Shepard."

"Well, we were passing by," Harriet explained, "and Gerard suggested we might drop in for a few minutes. . . . Oh, yes, thanks so much; a little scotch, if you have it."

Phil sprang to pluck the cat and a newspaper out of the chair she was about to sit down in, but that was the only awkward moment of the visit so far: Mrs. Talmage seemed accustomed to finding her ease almost anywhere.

"So how've you been, Phil?" Flash said quietly.

"Oh, not bad. How about you?"

"Good."

It couldn't have been easy for Ferris to arrange this reunion, and it was just like Ferris to assume that bringing the old lady along would give it more weight. Was Phil now supposed to say "Show you my room" and take Ferris upstairs? What kind of horseshit was this?

"Working hard?" Flash asked him.

"Well, putting in the hours, anyway. And the money's been nice."

"Good. Except I don't see any—"

"Don't see any what?"

"Well, never mind."

It seemed to Phil that he would never understand how he'd come to be standing here with one of the worst outcasts of the Irving School, each of them nursing a bottle of Coke, while an ill-assorted company of grownups pretended to enjoy themselves.

"How long were you in the navy, Captain?" Mrs. Talmage inquired.

And Charles's blushing, blinking embarrassment lasted only a second before he said "Well, no, I'm afraid that's a misunderstanding on Mrs. Drake's part. I was in the army, you see, and I've never—cultivated the term 'captain' in civilian life."

"Oh, I see," she said. "Well, most of the men in my family were naval officers. My father and grandfather were both rear admirals, and my husband retired as a full commander. He was on active duty for twenty-five years—much to my displeasure, I'm afraid. I can remember telling people he cared more about the navy than he cared about me, though even now I'd prefer to believe that was only a joke. Mostly a joke, in any case."

"Oh, that's charming," Grace Shepard said, with a fuzziness in her voice that suggested she was beginning to fade. Charles risked another look at her eyes, and there was the proof of it: they were still bright but were losing their life; she could still recognize a charming remark but in a few more minutes she wouldn't hear a shout. One good thing, though, was that she was seated in a deep old armchair with her head against the back of it: she might subside and pass out in all that upholstery without anyone's having to notice until the time came to rouse her for the taxi ride home— and by then, with luck, Mrs. Talmage would be gone.

"Philly?" Gloria called. "Why don't you take Flash out in the yard?" And she explained to Mrs. Talmage that the yard was really the nicest thing about this funny old damp house.

Phil had felt all summer that even if the yard could be purged of its rocks and humps and thistles, there would still be far too many years' worth of dead leaves in all directions for it ever to be nice. He had made a few stabs at cleaning up parts of it with the landlord's rake and lawnmower, but the tines of the rake kept getting ensnared in long, wet, weak strands of grass that made the sliding lawnmower almost useless.

Still, Flash Ferris apparently found it a good-enough set-ting for a conversational stroll. He seemed to know just what he wanted to say, and if the words were a little more nervous-sounding than he'd planned, their substance was clear and straightforward.

He said he didn't see any reason why Phil couldn't quit the parking lot and come on out for bike rides again. Wouldn't it be a shame to waste the last few weeks of their vacation? "And frankly," he concluded, "I haven't even been getting out of the house much any more. I mean it isn't any fun any more to go for rides alone."

Phil knew at once how easy it would be to demolish the argument with a quiet little snort of disdainful laughter, but that was the trouble: it would be too easy, considering how openly Flash had asked for it—and considering too that the poor bastard had so little time left to brace himself, with companionship, for his new start at Deerfield. Plainly, the better thing would be to reply with a carefully reasoned argument of his own.

"Well, but the point is I can't do that, Flash," he began, "because I'll need all the money I can make between now and September. I've got to buy a new tweed jacket—those things cost more than you might think, if you go to a decent store. And I need a lot of other stuff too: new pants, new shirts, new shoes . . ."

He was lying about all this—earlier in the summer his father had agreed to buy him the jacket and at least one new pair of flannel pants, if the shirts and shoes could wait until Christmas vacation—but the lies seemed well worth telling for Flash Ferris's sake. "And then if there's anything left over," he went on, "I'll need it for spending money. Last year I think I must've been the only kid in school that didn't have an allowance from home."

There was such a long silence then, as they paced the ruined yard, that Phil began to hope he'd said enough; but he hadn't.

"Okay," Flash said at last, "so how about this: I'll ask my grandmother to let you have two hundred dollars. Three hundred dollars."

And Phil was disgusted. The hell with trying to be nice. "Ah, Ferris," he said, "you're hopeless. Look, I'm gonna forget you said that, okay? Because it's just so dumb it's enough to make me puke. But I wanna tell ya something: if you go around propositioning people that way, at Deerfield or anywhere else, God help your ass."

"*Okay,*" Flash said in a wretchedly quiet voice. "*Okay; okay.*"

Phil was a little sorry for his outburst, if not quite sorry enough to take more than a glance at Flash's mortified face. He said curtly that he'd better go back inside and get ready for work now, and that was another lie because he still had hours to kill. But then, just before they reached the house, he gave Flash a qualified smile and a slow cuff on the shoulder, rubbing the knuckles in hard to acknowledge how foolish the quarrel had been, and Flash looked grateful and forgiving.

". . . Well, this was back when we lived in Pelham," Gloria was saying in one of her long, drink-thickened monologues. "Personally I would never've dreamed of moving to a barren little middle-class town like Pelham and I've had nightmares about it ever since, but the children's father happened to find a house for us there that year, you see, when we had nowhere else to go, so there we were. And I don't think Rachel really minded it—she's always been the most adaptable member of the family—but Phil seemed to hate the environment there as much as I did. I mean for one thing I was the only divorced woman for miles around and the neighbors were very 'kind' to me about it, if you can imagine anything worse, and Phil could sense all that . . ."

It was an anecdote Phil had often heard before, intended to show what a precocious little fellow he'd been at eight or nine, but he was fairly sure he could sidle around the party and get upstairs before she came to the climax of it.

"*Any*way, I'll never forget our Phil at that immaculate Pelham dinner table. He looked up at our host and said 'Is insurance all you ever talk about, Mr. Blanding?' "

But whatever hesitant chuckles she had won around the room were drowned in the deep and heavy rhythms of her own laughter.

Harriet Talmage was aware that Gerard had come to hover near the arm of her chair as a way of saying he was ready to go home, and she wished he were still small enough to be shooed away. She didn't feel at all like leaving yet, and probably wouldn't for quite a while, so it was a relief when he found a chair for himself against the wall.

She had taken a liking to this melancholy army man, with

his quiet wit and his furtive glances of hoping she hadn't yet noticed how stiff with alcohol his wife had grown. If it weren't for the wife—and perhaps the wife wasn't always this way—Harriet felt sure he would fit in admirably with her own small circle of friends.

"Where were you stationed in the service?" she asked him. "Were you overseas?"

"Well, only for a few minutes, so to speak, and that was very long ago. No, I spent most of my army years here in the States, and mostly in very boring—"

Rachel Shepard was suddenly up and striding for the kitchen, almost ready to cry, and she didn't care if everyone thought she was rude.

She had always despised her mother's Pelham stories because Pelham was where she'd met the only two dear friends of her life, Susan Blanding and Debbie Shields. They'd been as close as any three girls can be—sharing all each other's secrets, often "staying over" at one another's houses to try new hair styles, to talk far into the night and giggle helplessly about boys.

When Rachel left Pelham they all agreed it wasn't necessarily a tragedy, because they could write eagerly awaited letters of many pages apiece, and for a while they all kept that promise. Still, nothing as fragile as a three-way friendship can survive long spaces of time and absence, and Rachel hadn't heard from Susan or Debbie in years. She couldn't say what had become of them now, except that they'd both probably gone away to college somewhere.

Last winter she had written careful letters to each of them, addressed to their parents' homes, saying she was married to a wonderful man and expecting her first child; but she hadn't really expected either girl to reply, and neither of them did.

She had meant only to hide in the kitchen now until her mother's awful little gathering was over, but soon, impelled by a stronger and purer sense of rebellion than she'd ever known before, she left the house and started walking firmly toward the road.

She thought she had never seen an uglier, more brutal-looking man than the chauffeur who rested his rump against one fender of Mrs. Talmage's limousine. He watched her approach as if this were the first time he'd ever seen a pregnant woman; worse, his lewd stare seemed to be calculating how it might be to have her for himself. In order to keep her footing secure on the driveway, rather than risk a slip in the masses of dead leaves, she had to turn sideways and edge past him that way, facing him—this was horrible —before she could turn toward the road again and keep walking. She glanced back once to see if he was still watching her, and he was, and she trembled as if from a narrow escape. Down at the roadside she took cover behind a clump of evergreen bushes where the big tin mailbox stood (it was hardly ever used except for bills, because nobody could be expected to write letters to any member of this false, crazy family), but she didn't have to wait there more than a minute or two before Evan's car came along and slowed down for the turn. She took several clumsy steps into the road and waved him urgently to a stop with both hands, and he looked puzzled.

"Darling, I came to get you here because I can't bear to let you go into the house tonight, and I'm not going back there either. Listen—" The rest of her message was so rushed and jumbled she was afraid he'd tell her she wasn't making sense, but all he said was "Get in."

Then later, when he'd calmed her down with a gin and lime at an inexpensive restaurant they knew on Route Nine, she began to speak slowly and unemphatically enough for anyone's understanding.

". . . Because she really is crazy, Evan; that's what I've come to recognize. And I don't mean 'crazy' in any harmless or funny way, I mean out of her mind. Divorced from reality. Off in some other world of her own. Oh, I'll probably go on 'loving' her, whatever she is, but I can't *live* with her any more—that's the thing. So look." And Rachel leaned across the table to take his hand. "Whether it's fair to her or not, I think we've got to get out of that rotten old house as soon as we possibly can. *That's* what I wanted to tell you."

With his bright eyes narrowed in a smile of love, Evan raised his drink as if to propose a toast. He said he was very, very glad to hear her say all that. He said it was the best news he'd had in years; and now he had some pretty interesting news of his own.

Did she remember his mentioning Frank Brogan, at the plant? The guy who'd lent them the apartment in Jackson Heights that weekend, before they were married? Well, Frank would be getting drafted any time now—he didn't know how soon, because all the draft board could tell him was "any time"—and he'd offered to turn the place over to Evan as soon as he'd cleared out. Wouldn't that be a break?

"Because I mean a lot of guys going into the service are subletting their places for terrific profits, but Frank doesn't want to mess with any of that: we'd have the same rent he's been paying there for years. Oh, and I know you didn't much like the looks of it, dear, but we could change all that to suit ourselves—fix it up any way you want."

She agreed that getting Frank Brogan's apartment would be fine, though her memories of it didn't kindle much enthusiasm: a stark, threadbare, masculine place where she'd spent the whole weekend on the verge of hysteria, afraid of losing Evan forever if she couldn't overcome her fear of sex. Still, it was only an "any time" kind of thing; something better might easily turn up first.

When their dinner arrived—plates of lukewarm filet of sole with boiled potatoes—she settled down to tell him more about this galvanizing afternoon. ". . . Oh, and your mother's pickled, Evan. I mean I've seen her drunk before, but this is different: she's embalmed. It's like having to look at a corpse in an armchair. And your father can't even begin to get her home, you see, until this terrible old millionaire lady leaves—and the millionaire lady keeps staying and staying, talking and lapping up the booze. She must be seventy-five, but I think she's got as much of a yen for your father as my mother's ever had. Oh, and you can see my mother sensing the competition, too, rising to the—wait. Excuse me a sec."

Rachel went off to the ladies' room, holding the seat of her dress bunched oddly in one hand. She was gone a long time, and when she came back to her chair she looked very pale.

"Darling?" she said. "Listen: don't get scared, but I think I'm starting to have the baby right here in the restaurant. Isn't that ridiculous?"

13

A son was born to them at Huntington General Hospital, early the next morning. He was healthy and perfectly formed, and Rachel had what her doctor called an easy time of it, considering the birth was at least two weeks premature.

On Rachel's instructions ("I don't care if my mother *ever* finds out") Evan made the first phone call of the day to Curtis Drake, who said he hoped to be at the hospital by nine o'clock.

Then he called his own father, and he could tell at once that things weren't going smoothly at home.

"Well, that's—splendid news, Evan. I'll give Gloria a call, then, and I'll stop by her place and bring her on over there. That probably won't be until sometime sort of later in the morning, though, because there are still quite a few things to be done here. Your mother had a difficult night, you see, and she isn't feeling at all well."

Gloria wasn't feeling well either, though she was fairly sure she'd managed to convey the appropriate sentiments of joy on the telephone.

Years ago, and especially during Prohibition, having a hangover could be almost as much of an adventure as drinking itself: you could waste a whole day in absent-minded idleness, laughing easily and often with whoever you'd gotten drunk with the night before, mistrustfully sampling various kitchen "remedies" until the time came to agree, with all your heart, that a little hair of the dog might be the best thing after all.

Age and loneliness had spoiled all that. The only advantage now was that you knew what the best thing was from the start and didn't hesitate to make use of it. On any other bad morning she would have poured a decent amount of whiskey into a bedside glass, cut it with water from the bathroom tap, and swallowed it all before even trying to get dressed; but this would have to be a day of decorum. Clothes and cosmetics came first; then she went downstairs and made coffee, surprised at her own skill and patience, and she was able to force down nearly a cup of it before taking her medicine like a lady, with ice.

Now she could breathe again. She could gather her wits and wait for Charles's taxicab to sound its horn in the driveway. And she was ready for whatever little jokes might arise ("Well, but the trouble is I simply don't feel like a *grand*mother, Charles; can you help me with that? I don't even know how a grandmother is supposed to *feel.*")

"Evan said she had an easy time of it," Charles was saying, "though I don't suppose it can ever be called 'easy,' can it. Giving birth is one kind of suffering no man can ever claim to understand."

They were riding together into Huntington now on the slick, buoyant seat of the cab, in bright sunshine, and the funny part was that Gloria could have sworn she was still alone at the kitchen table with her medicine. Decorum or not, this was evidently going to be one of those addled days without regard for logical sequence, when small events and transitional periods of time were instantly lost to memory. It would be best not even to ask Charles if he could help her feel like a grandmother now because there was no way of knowing whether she'd made the same request at least once before, in the same words, back in the driveway or somewhere on the road. She would have to pay close attention to every moment from now on, or the whole day might get away from her.

One thing she noticed very clearly, and promised herself to remember, was that a tasteful-looking place called Crossroads Restaurant and Lounge lay less than a block from the hospital entrance. When their duties in the maternity ward were completed this morning, Gloria and Charles could drift as if by chance into the Crossroads Restaurant and Lounge for a few ice-cold martinis and a nice, light lunch.

"Why don't you sit down here, Gloria," Charles said in the swarming bewilderment of the hospital lobby. "I'll go find out where the maternity ward is, but it may take a minute in a place like this."

They were pressed into an elevator full of Negroes and cripples and fools, all holding hot paper cups of coffee and saying "Good morning" to each other as if it might be the last morning of the world. Then there were several corridors that led in wrong directions, and when they found their way at last into the nook where Rachel lay in a high stiff bed, there stood Curtis Drake.

He took Gloria wholly by surprise, in his dark little gabardine suit. She wanted him to vanish at once but he was here to stay, smiling, pleased with having brought the dozen roses whose nodding heads seemed to enhance the pallor of his daughter's exhausted face.

"Well, Gloria," he said. "Isn't this something? Isn't this great? And Mr. Shepard; how're you, sir?"

Rachel was still groggy but extremely talkative, and the first thing she wanted them to know was that Evan had stayed with her all night—he'd been a "lamb"; he'd left the hospital only a little while ago, to get to work. "And have you seen Evan Charles Shepard Junior yet? Oh, he's a beautiful boy. Go and look at him, okay? Ask one of the girls outside."

When a sterile-masked nurse held him up for their inspection through the plate glass he looked like any other infant—no better, no worse—with his head wobbling and his lips and gums stretched open in a cry of silence.

Neither Gloria nor Charles came up with anything trenchant to say about him, so they mumbled a few pleasantries and went back to Rachel's bedside.

". . . And we're never going to neglect him in any way, Daddy," Rachel was saying, "but we won't sort of impose ourselves on him either—we'll never let our problems be *his* problems, if you see what I mean. Well, I know it's silly to be talking this way when he isn't even half a day old, but I—"

"I don't think it's silly at all, dear," Curtis assured her. "I think it's grand."

Gloria took a look behind the hanging yellow cloth that was meant to insure semiprivacy, and there lay another girl or woman with her legs apart and her knees up so that anyone could see the sanitary napkin at her crotch.

"Oh, and another thing," Rachel said. "If he's very, very bright we'll always encourage him to make the most of his intelligence, and if he's sort of slow we'll never push him into more than he can—"

Something in her daughter's prattle had been irritating Gloria's nerves all this time, and now she could tell what it was: Rachel was talking with her molars clenched, either because she was still in pain or because she thought it might help keep her voice down in deference to her roommate behind the hanging cloth, and it made all her sibilants come out funny. Phrases like "most of his intelligence" and "if he's sort of slow" had a clicking, spitty sound that only Curtis Drake, in all the world, would ever consider grand.

"And we may have to move him around a lot," Rachel was saying, "because of Evan's education and career, but we'll never let him feel he doesn't have a home. We'll take our home along with us wherever we go because that's the kind of home it'll always be; do you see?"

"Well, sure, honey," Curtis said, "but don't you think you ought to get some rest now? We'll have plenty of time for talking later on."

"Oh, yes, plenty of time later on," Gloria said. "You'll have plenty of time for talking when her teeth aren't clenched against her mother, and that'll be grand indeed. 'Grand'—oh, what a simpering word that is, and my God, what a simpering little man you are, Curtis. Listen, Rachel—"

"Oh, no. Please," Rachel said. "Please. Daddy? Charles? Can you just sort of get her out of here? Can you get her out of here now before I—"

"Listen," Gloria said again. "Do you want to know why you and your brother've never had a home?"

"Oh, she *is* crazy, Daddy; she *is* crazy. If you can't get her out of here I'll get somebody to call the whaddyacallit, the psycho ward, and they'll put her in a straitjacket and lock her up. I mean that."

"You've never had a home," Gloria said, "because your father is a coward and a coward and a coward."

Curtis had taken one of her upper arms and Charles took the other. They walked her quickly out into the corridor and held her there, not knowing what else to do. She was both weak and powerful as she struggled in their grip, and her voice wouldn't stop: ". . . soft little cowardly swine. Oh, swine. Swine . . ."

"Can I help you?" a very young man inquired. He looked too young to be a doctor but he wore a stethoscope slung around his neck, as very young doctors often do.

"Yes, perhaps you can," Charles began. "We're looking for the psych—" and he would have said "the psychiatric facility here" if Curtis hadn't cut him off.

"No, this'll be all right. We need an elevator now, is all."

And from then on Curtis was plainly in charge. It was Curtis who got her into a mercifully uncrowded elevator— "coward; swine"—and he who steered her alone through the rushing employees and the standing wheelchairs and flowers of the lobby. In the dazzling light outside the main entrance he whistled up a cab for her and carefully loaded her into the back seat of it, saying "There, now; there now." Charles was needed only once, to recite her exact address in Cold Spring Harbor; then it was Curtis who pressed a five-dollar bill into the driver's hand and said "Just be careful with her, son. This lady's emotionally disturbed."

"She's what, sir?"

"Mentally ill. Got it?"

They went briefly upstairs again to comfort Rachel— "Well, it was sweet of you both to come back," she said, "but I'm fine. Really, I'll be fine now"—and afterwards the two of them strolled like friends into the shaded, air-conditioned barroom of the Crossroads Restaurant and Lounge.

"I thought you handled all that admirably, Curtis," Charles said. "If it had been left to me I might only have made things worse."

"Well, these—displays of hers can be very upsetting, but I've seen her through worse than this. She'll be very ashamed for a while and then she'll be well again—or at least as well as she's ever going to be. Besides—" And Curtis looked thoughtfully into his glass. "Besides, I think our friends in the psychiatric line still have a great deal to learn."

"Oh, I agree," Charles said. "Matter of fact, I couldn't agree more. I've had to take the same position with my own —with a member of my own family."

"Maybe someday I'll be able to trust the morbid little bastards—and I suppose the war is bound to teach them a few things—but not yet. Not yet. They're fooling around in the dark, is all."

"Exactly."

It wasn't until they were well into their second drinks, having happily agreed to stay here for lunch, that Charles Shepard said "You know a funny thing, Curtis? I don't even know what kind of work it is you do. I mean I know you're a business executive, of course, but I've never really—"

"No, 'executive' isn't quite right. I'm more on the level of a staff sergeant, you might say, than a commissioned officer. I work for Philco Radio, is all. Sold in the field for a good many years; then I came over into a job on the sales-management side. I'm one of four assistant sales managers for the area of greater New York."

"Well, that sounds very—that's really interesting. A good friend of mine in the army went into the radio business, back in about 'twenty-eight or 'twenty-nine, and I *think* it was Philco he started out with. I don't suppose you've ever heard the name—Joe Raymond?"

"No, I don't believe I have," Curtis said. "Still, there's

been quite a heavy—you know—quite a heavy turnover in sales personnel since 'twenty-nine.''

And Charles said he could easily imagine that must be true.

". . . So how was she when she got home?" Rachel asked her brother that afternoon. "She still out of her mind?"

"Well, I don't know. I mean I really don't know, Rachel, because I didn't see her. She knocked on my door and told me the baby was born, is all; then I got the bike and came right over here. She was in her room when I left, I think."

"Oh. Well, she might stay in her room for days and days now, trying to make us all feel bad because *she* feels bad. Daddy said she needs the shame of these things as much as she needs the explosions, only he called them 'displays.' He said it's a cycle he's known about since even before they were married. Oh, but look: let's not talk about this stuff any more, okay? I'm sorry I even told you what happened. So listen: why don't you go and have a look at your nephew. Just ask any of the girls out there. See if you don't think he's the image of his father."

"Well, good," Phil said. "I'll have a look."

Gloria kept entirely to herself for the next two weeks. From small remnants found in the kitchen every morning— a stain of milk or egg or meat on the linoleum counter—it was clear that she came downstairs to feed herself at night, but her bedroom had become her fortress and tabernacle, and except for an occasional creaking of floorboards it never emitted a sound.

"Oh, I know I could probably go in there and talk to

her," Rachel explained to her husband after the first week, "but I don't really feel like doing that. I don't want to."

And Evan's mumbled view, as he opened his newspaper, was that sometimes it was best to leave well enough alone.

"And then I keep wanting to call Daddy for advice on this, but that's pointless because I know he'll just say there's nothing anyone can do."

"Right," Evan said, rattling the paper firmly into reading position. "And besides, if you want to go around calling her crazy, you might as well let her be crazy."

Privately, Evan felt he couldn't be expected to pay much attention to any gloomy domestic crisis here when the real interests of his heart were miles away.

"Daddy?" Kathleen said during one of their Saturday rides together. "Mom says she and you are good friends again."

"Well, what's the matter with that, sweetheart? Whoever said divorced people can't be good friends?" And it was profoundly pleasing, as he reached from the steering wheel and tousled her hair, to know that only a few hours from now he would have her mother in his arms.

Phil Drake's fields of interest were divided now too. Ever since the night of Aaron's party he'd found himself on easy, jolly terms with the kitchen staff and the waitresses at Costello's. He didn't even have to eat at home any more because succulent suppers were prepared for him at work, with the manager's tacit approval ("Gotta put a little weight on this boy, right? Case we ever need him to defend our country?").

Shortly before dark one evening, as he walked glowing with food and camaraderie from the service door, he saw

Mrs. Talmage's limousine pull into the far end of his lot. Ralph drove as slowly past the few parked cars as if he were conducting a sight-seeing tour, and his two smiling passengers were Flash Ferris and a much smaller, younger boy.

"Just checking up on you, Drake," Ferris called as the limousine came to a stop. "Wanted to make sure you're hard at work here."

"Well, good," Phil said, fitting his cap carefully into place. "Glad you came by."

"This is Rod Walcott. He'll be starting in at Deerfield too."

"Hiya, Rod."

"Hi."

The boy was about twelve, barely of boarding-school age but squaring his shoulders and visibly trying to look older in Flash's company.

"Deerfield sent out this letter to all the new boys," Flash explained, "so we could get together if we wanted, and Rod's the only other one from this part of the Island. And I mean he's little, but you oughta see him on his bike: this kid can really travel."

"Good."

"Not much business here tonight," Flash observed.

"Well, it generally doesn't pick up until after dark; that's when I have to start hustling, if I want to make a buck."

"I see. Well; hope you make a whole lot of bucks."

Phil gave his flashlight a little end-over-end flip in the air and caught it neatly in his palm, as tennis players sometimes do with their racquets.

"So how about the Marine Corps, Flash?" he asked. "You still planning to try for it next winter?"

Flash blinked and ducked his head bashfully, seeming to shrink a little under Rod Walcott's incredulous stare; then he said he hadn't decided yet. He might do that, and he might not. He was thinking it over.

And just before the limousine drew away Ralph turned in the driver's seat to give Phil a slow, sardonic nod and a wink, making clear that he hadn't missed a nuance of the conversation. No weakness in the world, apparently, would ever be lost on Ralph.

Rachel had just fed the baby and put him down for a late-morning nap when she decided her mother's isolation had gone on long enough. Tiptoeing from the baby's room and closing his door, she knew at once how simple and natural a thing it would be to go and do something about the other closed door down the hall.

She checked the mirror first to make sure she looked all right—hair in place, face set in a pleasing expression of concern for another person's welfare—then she walked the distance to Gloria's door and gave it a sharp little rap.

"Mother?" she called. "I know you haven't been feeling well, but won't you come out and join us soon? We've all missed you."

This was substantially what she'd planned to say, except that the words "We've all missed you" seemed to have been spoken of their own accord, and as she waited for some response she braced herself for a heavy scent of rotten tomatoes or of old, rancid mayonnaise.

But the air in the room was surprisingly fresh—the open windows had provided cross-ventilation day and night—and Gloria's appearance was surprising too: she wore a clean, stylish summer dress, and except for a slightly truculent lift of the chin to suggest she had nothing to apologize for, her face could have been called serene. Clearly, though, she wasn't going to talk until Rachel did a little more talking first.

"I've just put the baby down," Rachel said, "but you'll see him this afternoon. See if you don't think he's changed a whole lot, just in this little bit of time. If he goes on changing at this rate we won't know *what* he's going to look like."

"Well, they all do that when they're new," Gloria said. "You changed a lot too, and so did Phil." Her voice was as hoarse as could be expected after two weeks of silence and many hundreds of cigarettes, but it held a tone of redemption: it seemed incapable now of the rancor and malice in her cry of "coward," or of any other kind of troublemaking.

"Can I fix you some lunch, Mother?" Rachel inquired. "Or something like that?"

When Phil got up and came downstairs that day he found the two of them seated together in the living room, murmuring and chuckling over the baby, and he didn't need any signal from his sister to know it would be best to act as if nothing had happened.

They were all waiting for Evan now. They needed his homecoming to settle their newfound peace of mind; and they felt lucky, when he came in from the car, that he appeared to be at his jaunty best.

"Gloria," he said. "Good to see you."

It seemed to Phil, though, that Evan's smile on finding her back in commission betrayed the look of a frugal young working man who hadn't forgotten which side his bread was buttered on.

"Well, I suppose we've had our ups and downs this summer," Gloria said when the drinks were served, "but *I* think we can all be happy here, don't you?"

14

Frank Brogan was drafted during the first week of September. On his last day at the plant he gave Evan Shepard a new set of keys to the Jackson Heights apartment, and he said "Let me have two more nights there, okay? Then you can move your stuff in whenever you're ready and it'll be all yours."

The words "whenever you're ready" were the only part of the deal that rode uncomfortably with Evan as he started home that afternoon—How could you ever tell when you were ready for anything?—and he thought it might be a good idea to stop off at his father's house and talk it over.

"No, Evan," Charles said as they sat facing each other squarely across the kitchen table. "I don't think this is a wise move at all. Gloria's going to take it badly, and I must say she'll have my sympathies. You'll be ducking out of your agreement with her; you'll be leaving her stranded here and probably broke as well; you'll be letting her down in ways even a normally stable person would resent—and what you have to consider is that she's not a normal person. If you'd seen her in the hospital that day you'd never question that again."

"Oh, I never have questioned it, Dad. But look: this was Rachel's idea. I'm just going along with it because I think she's right. Trying to live without any privacy was a dumb mistake from the start. We both want to put an end to it, and the sooner the better. Simple as that."

Steam from a pan of boiling carrots had clouded Charles's spectacles. He removed them and began wiping the lenses thoroughly with a paper napkin, and Evan noticed once again, as he'd noticed for years, that all the decisiveness could vanish from the old man's face when you caught him with his glasses off. There was nothing to fear in a face like that; there was hardly any "character" there at all.

"Well, Evan, you'll do what you want, as always. All I can do is watch and wait and wish you luck—though I wish I had greater confidence in your judgment. In the principles underlying your judgment, is what I'm trying to say."

The glasses were fitted back into place now, restoring Charles to himself. "But for whatever it may be worth," he said, "I can tell you this: hurting a sick woman like this, under these circumstances, is a thing I'd never do. It's a thing I'd never even consider."

"No, I don't suppose you would," Evan said. "But then, you'd probably never've gone into sharing the rent with her in the first place, right? So it's not your problem, is it. It's Rachel's and mine, right?"

"Is that my son out there?" Grace called from the other room. "Because I want to tell you something, young man. I don't care how important this conference of yours is, or how much money depends on it or anything else. I want you to come in here right now and give your mother a hug."

"Well, I think this is the saddest evening we've had all summer," Gloria said, "with Philly having to leave us tomorrow. Oh, but never mind, dear. We'll all be sad and we'll miss you terribly, but you must know how proud we are that you're doing so well at Irving."

And to all three of her listeners, seated and smiling around the living room, it was clear that her avowal of sadness was only a formality. Ever since she'd been released from hiding she had gone so happily about the business of her days that the very texture of her voice had taken on a new lightness and strength.

Clenching his fists, Phil stretched both arms wide in a pantomime of sleepiness and said he was glad to be through at Costello's. He could go to bed tonight and wake up at the same time as everyone else.

"Oh, and it's a nice evening for us too," Rachel said, making the circle of happiness complete. "Evan doesn't have to be at work until noon tomorrow because the plant'll be closed all morning for inventory. It's like having a little vacation."

"Wonderful," Gloria said. "Would anyone like more coffee?"

It wasn't until they were alone in their own room, getting ready for bed, that Evan had a chance to tell his wife about Jackson Heights.

"Oh," she said. "Well, I mean I know it's good news, and it's what we've been waiting for and everything; I just wish it didn't have to—"

"Didn't have to what?"

"I wish it didn't have to happen right now, is all. I'll sort of hate to tell her, is the thing."

"Well, you won't have to, dear: I'll do the talking for both of us. Be best to do it tomorrow night, wouldn't you say? After your brother's gone?"

And Rachel said she supposed so. She was sitting on the edge of the bed in a fresh blue nightgown, very slender again now and looking truly attractive, in her "perishable" way, for the first time in months. He was briefly tempted to make a nuzzling lunge for her, but that might only take the edge off the delicious plans they'd made.

"Gee, this is funny, though, isn't it," she said, "that I should feel so bad about something I know is good."

"You'll feel better in the morning," he assured her. "I imagine you'll feel better about a whole lot of things in the morning, after we've—you know—after we've taken a little inventory of our own."

They had kept a careful calendar. Tomorrow, according to doctor's orders, would be their first day for getting laid again in the regular way. And if love in the afternoon had always seemed even better than love at night, there were no words glorious enough for the way it could be in the later hours of the morning.

At breakfast, the young Shepards could scarcely refrain from giving each other long, significant looks, and Phil Drake couldn't help but notice they were holding hands tightly under the table.

At Gloria's customary signal of liberation—"Well, I'll clear away these messy plates"—they all stood up. The young Shepards lingered long enough for saying goodbye to Phil and wishing him the best of luck at school; then they seemed almost to dance upstairs in their eagerness for seclusion.

Phil allowed a decent interval to elapse—five minutes or ten—before going up to his own room and methodically packing his suitcase. But when he'd finished doing that he began to know, without doubt or trepidation, what he was going to do next. His plan and the execution of it were almost one and the same: walk up the hall, set the suitcase soundlessly on the floor, use one forefinger to part the dotted-swiss curtain against the pane of glass, and have a look.

Oh, Jesus, it was the loveliest and most terrible thing he'd ever seen; it was the source of the world; and his shame was so immediate that he let the fabric slip back into place after only a second or two.

Evan suddenly froze in her arms and said "Look!"

"Look at what?"

"Somebody's hand just let go of the whaddyacallit outside. The door curtain. I saw it move."

He had been almost ready to come, strong in the knowledge that he'd satisfied her, but it was hopeless now. All he could do was fall out of her and lie on his side, on his own ribs, breathing hard, and when he could speak again he said "So I guess your little brother likes to watch, doesn't he."

"Evan, I don't believe you really saw that," she told him; "I think you imagined it." But because she was breathing heavily too she had to wait a few heartbeats for her voice to come back. "Everybody knows it's easy to imagine things and then think they've happened." And she paused for breath again. "Besides, that's simply not the kind of thing Phil would ever, ever—"

"Wanna bet?" he demanded. "Wanna bet he hasn't been

standing out there all summer? Taking little peeks and playing with himself?"

"I'm not listening to any of this. I won't hear any more of this vile, horrible—"

"Who said you had to listen? Whoever said you had to hear?"

Then he was up and lurching around the room to pull on his factory clothes with an angry little excess of energy in the buttoning and buckling and the zipping up.

"I know what I saw," he said, "and I'm not about to forget it."

Phil Drake's final moments of leaving Cold Spring Harbor would always be blurred in his memory. He knew he must have hauled his suitcase downstairs fast because a station taxicab was already honking for him in the driveway; he knew he must have made a stop in the kitchen to accept one last sloppy embrace from his mother; then he was on the train and the whole rotten little town was far behind him.

"Well, I think these'll be—serviceable," Curtis Drake said in the early afternoon of that day.

"Oh, sure they will," Phil said. "They're fine. And thanks a lot, Dad."

"You're entirely welcome."

They were standing in blue-white fluorescent lighting at one of several "midtown retail outlets" in a chain of men's clothing stores often and loudly advertised on the radio. Curtis had easily persuaded his son that two new suits from a place like this would be a better deal than spending almost the same amount of money on a new tweed jacket—

especially since the old tweed jacket had now been made presentable again with the leather patches on the elbows.

The two suits, brown and blue, had begun to worry Phil a little because he suspected they might be all wrong for the Irving School; even so, they had the look of valuable merchandise in the salesman's quick hands as he folded them in a tricky way and nestled them one after the other into the tissues of separate, suitcase-sized cardboard boxes that were then lashed together with clean yellow twine.

Some of the floor men here might be slobs, lazy and rude in their work, making no secret of their wish for better ways to make a living, but this one understood the business. The money's changing hands and the cash register's ringing up of the total were never the end of your sale: it was the style and finesse you showed in the follow-through that brought the customers back; these things were important if you wanted to keep your bank account on the sweet side—if you wanted any more weekends in the Catskills with your girl before the army claimed your ass. The final touch in your performance was pure flourish: you reached beneath the counter and withdrew, as if from nowhere, a slim five-inch cylinder of spoolwood with small metal arms protruding from either end. You quickly bent the prongs to span the distance between strands of twine; then hook-snap at one end and hook-snap at the other: you could offer up a neat little carrying handle and the whole fucking transaction was over.

"Here you go, young man," he said, "and I think you'll get a lot of good wear out of these suits. Or no, wait—" And he tilted his head to one side to give Phil an appraising look. "Considering your age and your general build, you'll probably outgrow them before they get half the wear they deserve; am I right? What are you, fourteen?"

"I'm sixteen."

"Oh; sorry. Still, looking younger than your age is a

luckier thing than looking older, right? For example, I'm twenty-six and most people take me for over thirty—that could give me a few problems in later life, am I right?" And he turned his fading smile to Curtis. "Well, thank you again, sir. Very much."

As soon as they were out in the brilliance and roar of the street again, Curtis said "Well, I wouldn't feel bad, Phil, just because some clerk in a store makes a wrong guess about your age. You'll get your full growth soon enough, and you'll fill out too. Seems to me that ought to be the least of your worries these days. So. Want to head on over to Grand Central?"

What Phil liked best about the Men's Bar at the Biltmore, apart from the very name of it, was that nobody's age seemed to matter there in the brief and profitable seasons of traveling prep-school boys. Soon a tall, cold draft beer was set before him, at one of the little tables along the wall, and a double scotch, with ice and water, had been prepared for his father. Some things seemed never to change: the pallor and fatigue in Curtis Drake's face would always give way to a look of ruddy health after a few swallows of whiskey, and by the time of the second round there'd be a fine sparkle in his eyes, reminiscent of rare and unexpected Christmas mornings long ago.

"What's the matter, Phil? You're not still brooding about that little clothing-store clerk, are you? You don't want to let things like that prey on your mind. Matter of fact, I was hoping we'd have more time today, so we could talk at some length about this general business of your growing up. I know you can't make any plans now beyond school and the army—that's only reasonable, for as long as the war goes on—but I wonder if you're prepared to grow into a few responsibilities of another kind. What I'm getting at, Phil, is that your mother is a very fragile person."

"Oh, I know that."

"She's extremely insecure and childish; she's always had to depend on someone else for survival."

"I know all that, Dad; you don't have to explain this kind of—"

"Well, all right. But the point is, that burden's always been mine in the past, and now I'm trying to think about the future. It can't be your sister's responsibility because your sister has a family of her own, so I imagine it's going to be yours. Oh, I'm not saying this is anything that necessarily ought to—you know—ought to concern you greatly for the *present*, Phil, but it's something to keep in mind. All right? Are we agreed, then? Can I have your hand on it?"

"Sure," Phil said, and they shook hands as soberly as men closing a deal that involved a fortune, though Phil didn't yet understand the terms.

"And now," Curtis said, "if you don't mind my sitting here like a tired old man, I think you'd better make a run for it. Everything else can wait, you see, but a train doesn't wait for anybody."

And Phil made a run for it, hurrying down the Biltmore steps with his cumbersome luggage and out across the floor of Grand Central, getting through the right gate in the nick of time before it rattled shut.

As the sleek, quiet New England train drew out of the tunnel and swiftly past drab uptown tenement blocks, row on row of them, there was nothing for him to do but ride.

"Hey there, Drake."

"How's it going, Drake?"

It wasn't much, but a few other Irving boys were saying hello to him as they moved up the aisle in their search for clusters of happier Irving boys in the cars ahead. One of them even paused at his seat to ask how his summer had been, and called him "Phil."

But there were no further diversions after the first glimpses of green at the rim of Connecticut. Philip Drake

had peeked and seen his sister locked in copulation with
Evan Shepard this morning, and time might never diminish
the shame of it. He knew it was possible for shame to be
nursed and doctored like an illness, if you wanted to keep it
separate from the rest of your life, but that didn't mean
there'd be any way to keep from knowing it was there.

"Would you like me to heat up the roast lamb tonight,
dear?" Gloria asked later that day. "Or would you and Evan
rather have some chicken fricassee? That'd be just as easy,
really, because all I'd have to do would be—"

"Well, actually," Rachel said, "I don't think Evan and I'll
be eating here tonight, Mother; maybe you'd better just fix
something for yourself, okay?"

And before there could be any further questions she
escaped from the kitchen and went upstairs. Now that the
baby was here it was always easy to make these little es-
capes, but the baby was no convenience in the hours of
waiting for Evan to come home. And on this particular
afternoon her waiting held a special, unspeakable tension
that didn't begin to break until she heard his heavy shoes
on the stairs.

"See what I did, darling?" she said. "I brought up some
cold beer for us."

"Good."

"And I know you're anxious to get this whole thing over
with—I am, too—but I think it'll be better if we can talk a
minute first, okay?"

"Sure." He had slumped into a chair by the little hearth-
side.

"Would you like me to light a fire?" she asked him shyly.

"A fire? In this weather? You out of your mind?"

"Well, all right, but listen. I know you'll have to tell her
we need privacy and everything, because of course that *is*

the most important point; but whatever else you say, don't tell her about the door curtain this morning, okay? Don't tell on Philly."

"I'll tell her whatever has to be told, Rachel."

"All right," she said. "But if you tell on Philly I'll never—"

"Ah, you'll never what?"

"I'll never forgive you. I'll always hate you for it. And I mean that, Evan."

"Yeah, yeah, yeah." He got up, belched deeply, wiped his wet mouth on his hand, and made for the door.

The conference downstairs couldn't have lasted more than ten or fifteen minutes, and it must have been very subdued, because Rachel could hear neither of their voices as she sat twisting her hands and rocking in something close to anguish.

Then she stood up and went quickly to the door because Evan was back. He said it was settled; it was over and done with; he had told her mother they'd be out of here within a couple of days.

"How'd she take it?"

"Seemed to take it okay. Isn't a hell of a lot else she can do, when you think about it."

"Did you tell her about the—did you tell on Philly?"

He began to pace the floor, moving away from her, making her wait for the answer.

"Well, I meant to," he said at last, "and now I almost wish I had, but it wasn't necessary."

"Oh, thank God. Oh, thank God for that."

And he turned on her. "You're a funny kid, Rachel, you know that? You 'love everybody' all the time; you 'thank God' for everything—Christ's sake, you even thanked God the day the army turned me down. I mean you're a nice enough girl, but you're soft. You're soft as shit."

"That's not fair, Evan."

"Yeah, and there's another one: 'fair.' You really think anything's ever been 'fair' in the world? Because listen, kid, I've got news for you. There *is* no fair."

"You know I don't like it when you call me 'kid.' "

"Kid," he said with a vehemence that startled them both. "Kid, kid, kid and child, child, child. Now, why the fuck don't you leave me alone?"

"I'll leave you alone," she told him, "when you stop talking to me in this awful, hateful tone of—"

That was when he moved up close and hit her across the face. It was only a slap but it was hard enough to hurt his hand and turn her head sharply away, enough to send her a few steps back and sideways until the bed caught her and whirled her around and sat her down. She wasn't crying yet and she wasn't looking at him, but a dark pink blotch was spreading in her cheek, shaped like the map of Texas, and he knew he'd have to get out of here fast or he'd hit her again.

Driving was the best way Evan had ever found for recovering from rage—for putting his mind back in order and his nerves at rest. You couldn't be out of control when you had to control an automobile. Shifting and steering, paying attention to traffic lights and speed limits, you always knew it wouldn't be long before you were thinking rationally again and making rational plans.

His first rational plan tonight was to find a phone booth and say "Oh, Christ, Mary, I've got to see you; got to . . ." But he put that one quickly aside because other, better plans were already developing. This probably wouldn't be a good night for going to Mary's place; and anyway there'd be other nights, soon and often. The better thing would be to go home—or rather to go home a good many hours from now, after he'd soaked up enough beer to be heavy and solemn and sleepy when he hung his head to ask Rachel's forgiveness.

Soon he was seated among strangers in one of the old roadside taverns where he'd wasted so much time with other factory guys in the lost, drab years of living in his father's house. His craving for whiskey was keen but he knew better than to trust it: beer was what you needed at a time like this, and if each beer left you feeling it hadn't quite done the job there would always be more where it came from.

"Oh, my God," he said a few times, just under his breath. "Oh, my God, I hit my wife." Each time he said that he had to look quickly around the bar to make sure nobody had seen his lips move; then he subsided gratefully again into the beer. These hours of remorse could be patiently borne as long as he knew he was alone and unobserved, with his car waiting just outside the door like a concerned, attentive companion. When he was heavy and solemn and sleepy enough, the car would take him home.

Some summer after the war, when there'd be an abundance of gasoline again, he thought he would drive all the way to the West Coast—taking his time, seeing whatever seemed worth the sight. This had the feel of a fine, strong, liberating idea, but his imagination couldn't do very much with it until he had first resolved the beer-fuddled question of who would be riding in the car with him. Rachel and the baby? Mary and Kathleen?

And he was beginning to feel so strong and free now that it took him no time at all to decide. Assuming they'd have him—and why wouldn't they?—it would be Mary and Kathleen.

There would always be strength and freedom in knowing what you wanted—everybody knew that—and Evan Shepard knew it now in his blood and bones. He could afford to acknowledge, with a sobering nod at his reflection in the barroom mirror, that it wasn't going to be easy. There would be sorrowful, disorderly elements in that drive across America—persistent thoughts of Rachel and the baby might hamper him at every turn and sometimes even seem ready to crowd him off the road—but he knew they'd be obliged, eventually, to recede into the past. They would have to yield the right of way.

Rachel was reasonably sure he'd come home before morning, but in the meantime she would have to endure the night. She lay crying only intermittently, as though crying were a luxury she couldn't yet afford, and in one of the silences between spells of crying she heard an old, slow, defeated person coming upstairs. She knew then, listening to her mother walk away down the hall and close the door, that she would have to get up soon and go in there and comfort her. She would have to say how sorry she was for the way things had turned out, and that wouldn't be hard— the Drakes had always found their own kind of renewal in tearful apologies and expressions of love—but it would have to wait awhile now because the baby was awake.

When she'd cleaned and powdered him and changed his diaper she brought him back into bed with her to be fed. And almost before she knew it, while his small face worked and pulled at her breast, she was talking to him as if he were old enough to understand.

"Oh, you little marvel," she said. "Oh, you're a wonder, that's what you are. You're a miracle. Because do you know what you're going to be? You're going to be a man."